Born in Glasgow in 1935, Angus MacNeill graduated in English Language and Literature and went on to study Theology, before spending most of his working life relating to cross cultural situations. He lived in the Democratic Republic of Congo for over twelve years and in Thailand for six years, as well as visiting many other countries in his capacity as an executive of BMS World Mission. On retirement in 2000, he and his wife Carol returned to Argyll in Scotland, where he has been able to pursue his love of walking, reading and writing, as well as keeping up with their three children and families in both England and Australia.

PATTERNS OF HOPE

Angus MacNeill

Book Guild Publishing
Sussex, England

First published in Great Britain in 2010 by
The Book Guild Ltd
Pavilion View
19 New Road Brighton,
BN1 1UF

Typeset in Baskerville by
Ellipsis Books Limited, Glasgow

Printed in Great Britain by
CPI Antony Rowe

A catalogue record for this book is available from The British Library.

ISBN 978 1 84624 514 5

Contents

Acknowledgements

The nine short stories of this book are entirely fiction, so there can be no journalistic tracking down of the characters. Having said that, this does not mean that there is no reality to the situations that you will encounter in reading the book. Most of these have been harvested from my own experiences in meeting and living with people in different countries, listening to their stories and sharing, to some extent, in their lives. It is to these people, therefore, that I would like to pay tribute. They have been the inspiration behind the book and I have been no more than their mouthpiece to you. So, at the outset, I wish to acknowledge with gratitude the impact of all these people on my life and make this book something of a tribute to them.

My thanks also to Carol, my wife, whose original design of the nine interlinked Celtic circles provides a visual unity to the stories of the book and their life-enhancing values.

Finally, a special note of appreciation for all those at Book Guild Publishing who have guided my steps so expertly and given every encouragement in getting this book off the ground.

Angus MacNeill

The Rebound

. . . Freely we serve,
Because freely we love, as in our will
To love or not: in this we stand or fall:

John Milton,
Paradise Lost

When a thing has to be done, it has to be done. I've always said that. I still say it, as a matter of fact, although I've had to redefine what it is that needs to be done – if, indeed, it needs to be done at all. That sounds a bit complicated and backing-off, coming as it does from someone who prides himself on being a no-nonsense, straight-at-it, practical sort of person. Ask any of my friends and they'll tell you that's me. I like things to be simple and direct. Of course, there have been complicated, up-in-the-air things that I had to read and write when I was training to be a mining engineer, and I've put together masses of reports over the years, but a lot of that stuff was mining jargon that I simply mugged up and churned out. Shut your eyes, think of a number and it all appears on the paper in front of you, while you give most of yourself to watching TV or listening to the gabbling of a disc jockey on the radio.

Anyway, where was I? Things that need to be done. That's it. Sometimes it's no bother, but at other times . . . well, you can guess the hassle. Or maybe you can't. If you're one of the favoured few who leads a hassle-free life, let me assure you that being a mining engineer in the parts of the world where I have worked was rarely free of hassle. We had it all the time. Admittedly we were paid pretty well but it took it out of you. I've been completely washed out at the end of a project, extra deep wrinkles on my forehead and a bit less hair. That's when I longed just to state what needed to be done and go on and do it, without all the endless arguments, discussions and compromises that whittled away at the effectiveness of what we were trying to do. I found I needed lots of 'stiffeners' to get through things and that wasn't much good for the liver in the end. Mine's OK really, or at least not too bad, but there are other people I could tell you about who . . . but you don't want to hear about them. It's my special story that you're interested in, I think, or else you wouldn't have started reading all this.

Well, that's two paragraphs of padding already, like the stuff you pack round explosives before they go off. Because something did happen to me that blew me off course – or maybe back on course depending on your point of view. You be the judge. I'll try to tell it as it is, dipping into my diary of events from time to time, just to make sure I've got the sequence right. There was an official log of events that I had to write up, but I kept an unofficial one as well which was a bit more revealing. The first gave the bones of what happened. The second added the flesh. The first I called the OLE (Official Log of Events) and the second was the ULE (Unofficial Log of Events).

I wasn't too surprised when I was told what was next on the agenda for our mining company. It had been talked about for long enough as 'the big breakthrough' for us, if we managed to pull it off. The trouble was political and until that was sorted out we were stymied. I wasn't involved in all that stuff, fortunately – no one sees me as a smooth diplomat – so I don't know all that went on. But in some ways it was obvious what was going to happen in a country with rich mineral resources and a disastrous economy getting worse by the minute. Time to cash in on the underground bank balance, and who better to help them do this than our company? A few personalised incentives to some people at the top, a list of side-benefit financing for all sorts of dream development projects, relentless pressure to get some signatures before our competitors really got to work, and we were home and dry. Champagne all round, lots of press releases and photos, and a phone call to me to pack my bags again.

There's no doubt the place was attractive. When I got there and saw the hills and the lake I said to myself that this could have been developed into a delightful tourist centre. A nice place. The only setback was that it was miles from anywhere in a country whose tourist facilities were near zero. There were people there, of course, but only locals. As I was to find myself being told time and time again, they had been there for gener-ations – farming, fishing, building their villages, living quietly, marrying, having children, being buried on the spot and so on. You know the sort of thing. It always comes up and makes for the hassle I was talking about earlier. And right at the centre of the site that had been given to us to mine was a village. I groaned when I saw it, because I knew it meant trouble.

Somewhere on page 73 or wherever of the agreement signed between our company and the government of the country, there was a section on this village. It wasn't complicated. The village was to be moved to another place. Houses would be built, a school and medical centre would be provided and possibly even an electric power line laid down. Who would look this particularly attractive gift horse in the mouth? No one, you would think. But you'd be wrong and I certainly wasn't taken in. That's why I groaned.

My first entry in the OLE – the Official Log of Events – was as follows:

24th July – Arrived at the site to be developed. Everything as it appeared in the planning document. No abnormal problem immedi-ately in view. First task will be clearing the village using normal methods.

On the other hand, the ULE was a bit more honest:

24th July – Lovely place. Village bang in the centre of our conces-sion is going to be a headache. I've got a bad feeling about it.

Of course, I didn't speak the local language, so when I visited the village the day after my arrival I was accompanied by an interpreter. He was supposed to be neutral when it came to any discussions, but how could I tell what twist he was putting on things that I said? I just had to trust him, and since I am not much into trusting anybody the length of my little finger, this didn't put me in a good mood. If it had been left to me, I would just have sent a message to the village that they had to be out and away within twenty-four hours, at the end of which time the bulldozers would move in. But company policy required me to take time over it – one of the compromises made by our 'company diplomats' in striking the deal with the government, no doubt.

The village was assembled to meet me when I arrived, accom-panied by the interpreter, a government official and a posse of armed policemen. This wasn't the first time that the villagers had met with the company and they knew exactly what had been decided for them. In me they saw the beginning of the end of their village. Lots of our mining equipment had begun to arrive in the area ready for the starter's whistle to blow. I had that whistle. I could feel all eyes focused on me as I sat down beside the local headman and stared out at the circle of villagers all around – men at the front, women standing behind.

I sat listening as proceedings dragged on. 'Listening' is hardly the word for it, since it was the usual rigmarole that I had heard many times before: 'Our ancestors lived on this piece of land. They are buried here. We don't want to go to the area that you say we are being given.' On and on it went. The government official and the villagers got into a heated argument. They began to complain that they had never been properly consulted and who was it that agreed over their heads to surrender their land to the mining company? I said we had a week to sort things out and we agreed – although 'agreed' was not the word I would have chosen – to meet again.

The OLE for the 25th July read:

First meeting held with the villagers. Everything going according to plan. One or two minor points to settle over the coming week.

Whereas the ULE read:

First meeting a real pain. Waste of time. Why can't people see which side their bread is buttered on? You'd think we were talking about knocking down the Sphinx or the Taj Mahal. For pity's sake, it is only a collection of ramshackle houses.

Then the worst happened. I was sitting in my 'office' a couple of days later – we had set up some rather nice temporary accommodation for ourselves down near the lake and my office window had a superb view over the water – when I was informed that I had a visitor. When he came in, I thought he was another government official. He had that look about him. Neatly dressed and carrying a businesslike attaché case. He spoke English with quite a polished accent. Having heard that I had arrived, he said, he had hurried from another part of the country to meet me. So sorry not to be at the village on the 25th for the meeting with the villagers. His village, in fact, although he didn't live there any longer, but his parents and grandparents did. My heart sank when I heard this. This was all we needed – some bright, articulate 'village lawyer' sort of person to put a spanner in the works.

Well, you don't need me to tell you what he was on about. It was the same old thing, but said in a calm, educated, yet forceful way, appealing for what he called 'a sense of moral responsibility' on the part of the mining company, who perhaps didn't understand what it meant for people to give up the land that their ancestors had nurtured since the year dot . . . and much more along the same lines.

'So what do you want me to do about it?' I asked at last, after listening to this harangue, which wearied me from the word go.

'Reconsider the location,' he replied. 'Move somewhere else, if you must, where you don't upset a community in the way that you are planning to do.'

'Show me that place,' I laughed impatiently, 'the place that isn't spooked by people's ancestors.'

Eventually I had to resort to saying that I had some pressing matter to attend to, and he left. As he did so, he said that he was sure we would be meeting again. *'You bet, we will,'* I said to myself rather grimly, knowing that this sort of interfering person wouldn't give up easily. That night the entry in the OLE read:

28th July − Arrival in the area of an articulate objector to the removal of the villagers to a better location. Has relatives in the village. Will need care in dealing with him, in order to avoid an unnecessary setback.

In the ULE for the same date I wrote some rather strong words, followed by:

A jumped-up relative of folks in the village came to see me today. Could he talk! Whoa! Tried to get me arguing about morality − as if I would be into that, when things that have to be done have to be done. The sooner we get the bulldozers in the better, before this fellow stirs things up.

I met with the villagers again on the 30th July. Who do you think was there? You're right – my friend with the attaché-case, except that this time he didn't have it with him and his smart clothes had been exchanged for something nearer to ordinary village dress. Right from the start the headman deferred to him and he became the spokesman for the village, sometimes speaking in the local language and being interpreted – the interpreter was a bit uneasy about that, I saw – and sometimes addressing me directly in English. We went over all the old ground, but I insisted that the agreement – which of course was for their wellbeing (I laid that on pretty thick, I can tell you) – could not be gone back on.

Stalemate. They said they wouldn't move voluntarily (led by Mr Attaché-case, who by now was receiving loud mutterings of approval every time he spoke). I said that the land would be cleared in two days' time on the 1st August, by compulsory eviction if necessary.

For the OLE that night I had to register a problem, but keep the panic out of it:

Some reluctance being shown by the villagers to moving. Being led by the 'articulate objector' (see log for 28th July). Confident the matter will be resolved amicably by the deadline of 1st August.

In the ULE I wrote:

The chips are down. We will move in on 1st August in force. With our 'village lawyer' whipping things up there is no chance of a peaceful exodus by the villagers. Would be helpful if he wasn't there on the 1st.

He came to see me on the afternoon of the 31st July. A last ditch effort to get me to change the deadline and give time for more discussion to resolve the problem. I told him that as far as I was concerned there was no problem. But he would have none of that. I told him his parents would be living in a better house than they had ever had before and that went for everybody in the village. He said that wasn't the point. We were back to the old story about the precious land that had come down from the ancestors and the obligation they had to care for it. I said the ancestors would have been over the moon if they had known prized minerals lay beneath the surface, which a skilled mining company like ours could come along and extract for the benefit of many people. But he scorned that reply of mine and spoke rather caustically instead about the mining company's profits.

This went on for half an hour, with me trying not to lose my temper. It just about snapped, all the same, when we got back to his favourite stamping ground about the morality of our actions and he said, 'As I stand before God, I believe you are acting wrongly.'

I wondered where he got the fancy phrase from – 'As I stand before God'. One of his books, I suppose. Anyway, I replied, 'What's God got to do with all this?' and he said, 'A lot, I would say.'

Well, I mean, I wasn't going to have this young upstart preaching at me. I told him we had talked enough. He left soon after that. The deadline for the next day remained in place.

Once he had gone, I did a bit of serious thinking. It didn't take a great deal of imagination to foresee what would happen if we went into the village to remove people and he was there protesting and stirring people up. Things could turn nasty and that was the last thing we needed. So, what to do? I recalled what I had written in the ULE the previous night about wishing that he wouldn't be there. That was the solution – more necessary than ever after all that had just passed between us in our conversation.

As I have said several times, when a thing has to be done it has to be done. So I got on the phone to see if something could be arranged. It was. The last thing some of the top people who had benefited from our generosity wanted to see was a messy clearance of the village and the whole thing getting publicised in some way. That's always a danger in the news-hungry world we live in, with the media gathering like vultures whenever they think there's a juicy story to cover.

I don't know what they managed to concoct, but my attaché-case carrying friend found himself in the local jail. I had a visit from the government official to tell me this, just in case I thought this would cause a problem the next day when we moved in to the village. He said this without a trace of a smile or smirk on his face. Sometimes I find that by the time you've finished double-talking your way through a situation like this, you're not too sure what's the real thing and what's made up. I assured him that I didn't think it would be any problem at all.

'As it happens,' I said brightly 'it might even be a help to us.'

So it was with some satisfaction that I logged the achievement in the OLE for that night:

All ready for the clearance of the village tomorrow. No problems on the horizon. The articulate objector has decided to remove himself from the scene, I am told, following our frank discussion of this afternoon, when I carefully explained the benefits to the community of what we were about to do.

In the ULE I merely made the comment:

> *How strange. My wish not to have 'attaché-case' around tomorrow has been fulfilled. A couple of nights in the clink will be a wonderful experience for a young man learning the ropes of real life.*

What I didn't know – hand on heart, I am being completely honest here – was that there had been some bungle in the arrest and an over-enthusiastic policeman had managed to break our friend's left arm. I only learned that later. These things happen, I suppose. News about it only got to me a couple of days later after the village move, plus the fact that they had really gone to town in getting 'attaché case' away from the area by flying him out somewhere – I never learned where. All this was a bit unfortunate, and went beyond what I had planned. I had no real hard feelings towards the young man.

I didn't go to the village on the 1st August. The big move could easily be attended to by others. Instead I got on with the chore of dealing with a mountain of paperwork that had built up in just one week. That's another hassle I have – the battle with paper. Ploughing through all that sort of stuff can really get me feeling depressed. The one compensation that day was the view over the lake. Absolutely wonderful.

Around midday a work colleague came to tell me about the village move.

'Is it completed?' I asked.

'Yes, but there were . . .'

'OK, I don't need to hear the gory details. All I'm interested in is whether the site is now cleared for action,' I butted in. I didn't want to hear who objected, and who cried, and who cursed, and so on. Give them a week in their new location and they'd be giving a party to all and sundry, I reckoned.

'It's clear,' my colleague replied with a shrug.

In both the OLE and the ULE for the night of the 1st August I had the satisfaction of recording the successful completion of the village clearance with no damage to anybody's life or limb. My ego was massaged by a congratulatory phone call from one of the company's vice-presidents, who expressed his relief that all had gone well and that there would be no adverse publicity.

'Care and patience. That's the way to do it,' he said. 'Care and patience.'

I said that I couldn't agree more.

I gave the new village time to settle down before going on an official visit. I see from the OLE and ULE that it was the 16th August, a good two weeks after the move. The visiting group was made up of more or less the same people who had been with me when we visited the old village prior to the clearance, – the government official, the interpreter and the posse of policemen. Of course, quite a bit still needed to be done in the new village itself, but I thought things were coming along quite nicely. Certainly the houses were much better built, and I saw the site for the new school and medical centre. We didn't have an official get-together with the villagers, but merely walked around in the company of the local headman. He didn't have much to say to me, and answered my questions with a fair bit of surliness, I thought.

We were just nearing the end of the visit when we were accosted by an old woman who seemed very worked up. The policemen tried to hustle her out of the way, but I said to let her have her say. And what exactly was she saying, I asked the interpreter? Apparently she was asking about why 'attaché case' had been arrested – at least that was what the interpreter told me. I told the interpreter to say how sorry I was to hear what had happened, and that I only learned about it on the day of the move and it really had nothing to do with me. However, the local government official was here and she would need to raise the matter with him. I think the interpreter must have translated exactly what I said, because she seemed to get the message. But instead of saying anything to the po-faced government official, who was carefully avoiding looking at me, she suddenly leapt forward before anyone could stop her and spat at me, shouting, 'You . . . You . . . You,' in English, over and over again.

She got a cuff on the side of the head from a policeman which sent her spinning. I had to intervene to stop them doing anything else.

'No!' I said. 'Leave her. She's old and upset. Not everyone can take change very well.'

It turned out this old woman was 'attaché case's' grand-mother. 'A life-long enemy there, I'm afraid,' I said to myself with a rueful smile.

For the 16th August, I wrote in the OLE:

Everybody settling down well in the new village. The move is a big success and people are showing themselves to be very enthusiastic about the future.

In the ULE, I wrote:

I don't like getting spat at, even by an old woman, but if you do things in certain ways, then I suppose this is the risk you run. Can't blame her too much. Presume the young man is OK, but no word on that front.

What happened next was about ten years later, after I had left that particular mining company. Incidentally, it made a huge profit out of mining the site on which the old village had stood. No surprise there. I mentioned earlier that my liver was more or less in good shape, unlike those of other people I knew. Well, that wasn't exactly the truth, so I'm going to be honest with you now. It got into a bit of a mess. All the hassle and tension and pressure – well, I used to unwind by drinking a bottle or two. Once you get into that habit, it escalates and you end up with a damaged liver and a damaged career. To add to it all I was getting older, and finding it difficult to keep up with all the bright young geeks coming up behind me with their boundless enthusiasm and smart ideas. So the company and I said goodbye to each other.

I knocked about for a bit here and there in different parts of the world, pay forever decreasing, until finally I found myself back in the country where this story is set. I got a job teaching in a technical college, and when I wasn't trying to explain fairly basic physics and geology to the students, I sat back and had a bottle or two. The trouble is that when you get into that way of life, you begin to get careless. And I was careless, not just when sitting on my small veranda with my feet up but, more seriously, in the classroom where I taught. My 'may-the-devil-take-you' attitude got the better of me.

I can't remember the whole thing very clearly, although later I was told many times what I had said. Apparently I made some sneering, half-intoxicated remarks about the president of the country. I think I said something about him having a face like a demented monkey. I must have been suicidal. There was a near riot in the class. At 10 p.m. that night they came to pick me up. I was bundled into the back of a car. They never said who they were, but I didn't need them to enlighten me. 'Secret police' was written all over the way they acted and spoke. They were rough, but not excessively so, and on hearing why they had come for me, I hoped a quick and sincere apology on my part would do the trick. Unfortunately it didn't. I found myself locked up in a large room with another twenty or thirty people.

I expected to be called out for interrogation every now and then, in the way that these things are supposed to go. It didn't turn out that way, apart from an initial run-in with somebody who looked as though he was in charge – not a great success because at that time of night I was pretty well sozzled. I was just left in this room with all the others. Some of them had been there for months, with no idea what was going to happen to them. We were like people dropped into a black hole, out of sight and out of mind of the world that we knew. Some were resigned to their fate, others less so. The general opinion was that, as a foreigner, I would probably get out alive, since somebody must know that I had disappeared, but who could tell? I got very depressed, and to make things worse there was no bottle handy to help me climb out of that depression.

To my relief, after I had been there for the best part of two weeks I was informed that my embassy had tracked me down. I was allowed to see somebody from the embassy who brought me some clean clothes and a few goodies. Things began to look brighter. But then another couple of weeks elapsed and I heard nothing. To make matters worse I was moved to a different place, along with five others whom I knew were 'in things' up to their necks. Not a good development.

Then one morning I was told that I was to see someone important. I was taken away from the others and made to wait outside another room for a few moments before the door opened and I was told to go in. There were two men seated there. One was in uniform – some sort of policeman I guessed – and the other was in ordinary but very smart clothes. My heart sank when I saw him. It was 'Mr Attaché-case' himself. Older, of course, but unmistakably him.

'Ah! We meet again,' he said.

I said nothing, but managed a twisted sort of smile.

The uniformed man then told me this was an important government minister, who had sought and received the permission of none other than the president himself to come and see me. I mumbled that I was honoured, although that didn't seem to cut much ice with either of them. They probably thought I was being cynical. If so, they were right because I couldn't see much good for me coming out of this honoured visit. However, at that point the uniformed man got up and said that he would leave me with the minister for a few moments.

So there we were, together after all these years. The last time I had seen him I had been ushering him out of my office before picking up the phone to have him arrested. What was there to say? How nice it was to see him or how were his parents or was his feisty grandmother still alive? That sort of approach wouldn't get me very far, I reckoned. Nor could I find it in me to grovel before him and say that I was sorry for what I had done. I wondered if he had come to see me in order to gloat over my predicament and rub a bit of salt into my wounds. If he felt the same way as his grandmother had done all those years ago, then I reckoned I might be in for a torrid time. I waited on him to make the first move. He must have guessed what was passing through my mind. It would have been easy for him to have got some pleasure out of keeping me in suspense for a few moments. But he didn't do that. He was quick to begin speaking.

'I've arranged for you to be released into my care until we can fix up a flight for you to return home to your own country. I'm afraid that is the reality of the situation, but it will be my delight to have you stay with us for a few days. I'm sure you must be longing for a proper wash and nice meal. Being in prison isn't very pleasant, as I know.'

He made that final comment with a slight raising of the eyebrows. I knew then that everything was going to be all right. That night I slept in a real bed – washed, clean and properly fed for the first time in a month.

We had plenty time to talk before I boarded my flight back home. Eventually I got round to trying to excuse myself as best as I could for what had happened all those years back. Frankly I made a poor job of it. It had been a cynical, mean manoeuvre on my part. The result for him had been that he spent nearly three months in some grotty prison before being released, and I could see that although his broken arm had mended it had not been a brilliant fix. He held his arm awkwardly. His painful experiences, which I had brought about, had been a lot worse than my short time in custody. All the more reason to be surprised by his help to me now.

I said something of this to him, before saying, 'God, you must have hated my guts for what I did.'

He shook his head and asked me, 'Isn't there something somewhere about loving your enemies and doing good to those who hate you?'

'Yes,' I said, 'but . . .'

He interrupted me, and said with a quizzical smile, since he knew quite well my philosophy of life, 'You can't really have any "buts", you know. What has to be done, has to be done.'

'Touché,' I said.

Textual Confusion

My prime of youth is but a frost of cares;
My feast of joy is but a dish of pain;
My crop of corn is but a field of tares;
And all my good is but vain hope of gain.
The day is past, and yet I saw no sun;
And now I live, and now my life is done.

Chidiock Tichborne

He who binds to himself a joy
Doth the winged life destroy
But he who kisses the joy as it flies
Lives in Eternity's sunrise.

William Blake

Going into bookshops was more or less an addiction, Judy would have been the first to admit. Whether it was an upmarket or a second-hand bookshop, or even just a charity shop with its two or three shelves of cast-off books, she couldn't resist going in to have a look around. More often than not, she came out with a book in her bag, feeling a little bit guilty that she had succumbed yet again to what she laughingly called her chronic 'bookitis'. It was during one of those quick in-and-out forays into a charity shop that she came upon Dominique Lapierre's 1980s book on Kolkata (or Calcutta as it used to be called then). For some reason she had never read it, although she knew a film had been made of it, and so the title *City of Joy* was well enough known to her. It was a good find, she thought to herself, and she looked forward to reading it.

Looking back, Judy always said it started from that point, although that was obviously something of an exaggeration. Probably it was more like striking a match to a heap of dry leaves that had been collecting over the years, waiting for their moment of ignition. Now Judy was no stranger to joy in life. Behind the book-loving Judy there lay no hidden, tormented soul with a history of dreadful experiences. Judy had had an idyllic, joyful childhood. She had always been happy and now that she was in her late twenties, she remained an open, outgoing sort of person with a bubbly personality.

Judy's childhood and adolescence were a picture of contentment. A stable family life with parents who loved her, and siblings who held together despite the inevitable frictions of growing up alongside each other, meant that she had ended up with a very positive outlook on life. She had always been an attractive-looking child and as adolescence progressed she grew into an even more attractive young woman. She was not overly 'body conscious' but she knew that nature had endowed her with a good thing, and she was not short of admirers who sometimes told her so to her face or implied it in their looks. Along with her attractive appearance there went a quick mind and she had had little difficulty in getting a good degree and a satisfactory, well-enough-paid job afterwards. Along the way she had had one or two boyfriends. To be frank, maybe that was the one area that had proved something of a disappointment.

'It's a bit like eating an apple,' she would say to her friend Kate. 'You take a bite and it tastes lovely and just at the point where you think you'll go the whole way and eat it all, you come across a really bad bit that has you spitting everything out into the sink.'

Apart from that, Judy felt that life was there for the taking and she looked forward to taking it with a smile – and a wiggle of her hips, if that was necessary. Whenever there was a slightly down moment – and they did come along from time to time – this could be got over by opening the pages of a book and escaping inside a story. This brings us back nicely to where we began, the purchase in a charity shop of Dominique Lapierre's book, *The City of Joy*.

Well, you know what happens. Anybody suffering as Judy was from 'bookitis' is more than likely to buy a book and leave it somewhere around the house on a pile of 'to be read' books. This is exactly what Judy did. She was going through one of her boyfriend phases, which distracted her from reading. In fact, it was only after this boyfriend had moved out of her life, and there was a bit of a gap in things, that she reached out to the 'to be read' pile in search of an escapist book as emotional therapy.

'It wasn't that I was really down or anything like that,' she said later to Kate, 'but you know how it is.'

Kate said she did. Having lived through this experience with Judy several times before, she was sure Judy would bounce back to her normal self in two or three days. Having said that, Kate couldn't help wondering if a little bit of permanent damage hadn't been done, and something of an edge hadn't been taken off Judy's bright and cheerful outlook. She caught Judy one evening sitting looking out of her window, staring into empty space, miles away.

'There's something going on in there,' Kate said to herself, 'but I bet you Judy won't admit it.'

And she didn't. Everything was fine according to Judy. Absolutely fine. No problems and very glad to be rid of the boyfriend. Give her time to do some things she had been meaning to do, such as reading a new book. Kate suspected that, to cover her embarrassment, Judy just reached out at that moment and, quite by chance, happened to find her hand gripping *The City of Joy*. However, once gripped and withdrawn from the pile, that became the book of the moment for her.

Dominique Lapierre's story of Hasari Pal, a rickshaw puller in Kolkata, moved Judy in a way that she had not been before, at least not for a long time. She was, of course, used to seeing TV clips of people living in appalling situations, mainly in Africa, but like many others she had developed compassion fatigue. Reading a book was different, Judy always said, and Dominique Lapierre's story did for her what no TV film had been able to do. For the duration of the book, she lived in Kolkata.

By now you are probably guessing what happened next. Kate was only mildly surprised when Judy told her that she was going to take some holiday due to her and go and visit Kolkata. This decision, as Kate saw it, was on a par with the way Judy lived her life generally – forever leaping from experience to experience like a bee going from flower to flower in search of the best nectar.

In the run up to her holiday Judy had the usual hassle over medical things, as well as getting a visa, and finding accommodation for herself in India that promised to be clean and not too expensive, but these things didn't tax her too much. Of more trouble was giving a reason for her journey to people who kept on asking her, 'But why Kolkata?' She herself wasn't too sure that she had it all worked out and so she would just smile one of her well-practised charming smiles and reply, 'Why not?' That seemed to do the trick.

She actually flew to Delhi first and spent two or three days there seeing the usual tourist sites. The bit of the city that she was in seemed very modern, although a short journey in a three-wheeled taxi-scooter was something else. She told Kate in a text message *Scooter ride 2 Red 4t – survived – unforgettable.* From Delhi she flew on to Kolkata, with a view of the distant Himalayas to the north. The taxi ride in from Kolkata's airport to the centre of the city had her glued to the window, as modern and ancient India went past in a chaotic jumble of buildings, people, animals and dense traffic. She found herself catching a whiff of Hasari Pal's city. It felt good to be there.

She had arrived in Kolkata with a phone number which she hoped would be her passport to a real experience of the city. A friend of Kate's had given it to her. The morning after she arrived, she picked up the phone in her hotel bedroom.

'Of course, please come and see us. Today if you like. I'll give you the address for the taxi driver.'

So it was that later that afternoon Judy found herself at the home of Ashish and Rani. It was something of surprise. They lived in an apartment belonging to a Christian organisation that owned a piece of land in central Kolkata. It was a walled-in property with a bit of grass and greenery to it, which made it like an oasis of peace in the middle of the dusty, congested and noisy city. Ashish and Rani couldn't have been more welcoming and they remembered Kate's friend quite well from when he had been with them for several months a few years back, doing some volunteer work in the city.

In some ways Judy was a little disappointed, because her image of India was of a Hindu country with a large Muslim minority and she wondered if meeting Christians straight away wasn't going to skew her understanding of things. Still, you couldn't quarrel with Ashish and Rani. They seemed very genuine, nice people and as Indian as you could get. Then, of course, there was Karl. *Kkata fascinating + Swede blond giant* she texted Kate, who gave a half laugh and half groan when she read it. The Karl in question was a volunteer like Kate's friend and he was there along with three others – a couple of girls and another fellow who was very nice, but not in the same class as Karl, in Judy's estimation. But to give her her due, Judy knew that she was in Kolkata for much more than a 'holiday fling' – she had had these in the past and knew that they were always a bit of a let down. 'Deflation after exhilaration' is how she used to describe it to friends.

Rani arranged to meet Judy in a couple of days' time and show her Kolkata, reminding her politely not to wear skimpy clothes, despite the heat.

'In any case,' Rani said, 'we'll probably be in some quite dirty places, so you don't want to get your nice clothes spoiled.'

This was the sort of thing that Judy had hoped would happen and so, despite some trepidation about what she would see and the effect it would have on her, she looked forward to their outing together. That night she texted Kate again – *Going out town w nu frend Rani* – which made Kate breathe a sigh of relief. No sign of the giant blond Swede.

When she spoke about it later, Judy could never remember all that she saw that day. It was such a jumble. The streets seemed to heave with life and movement. Open-fronted shops spilled out onto the pavement. Stalls or simple displays of fruit and vegetables, and household nick-nacks of all sorts, turned walking along the pavement into an obstacle course. And there were people, and yet more people. Some men smartly dressed in white shirt and trousers; others in traditional loose Indian dress; women in their saris; and for everybody a whole range of wealth on display – from obviously better-off members of the Indian middle class, to the destitution of the poor and the beggars. Added to it all was the noise of cars and buses and horns and the pervading musty, sweet, sweaty smell that seemed to hang over everything in the heat. One image that did remain with her from that walk through the streets with Rani was of a man carrying a leg of meat on his shoulder with a crow perched on it enjoying a quick snack on the move, before a jerk of the man's shoulder shook it off.

Rani said that Judy would find it easy to visit the better-off parts of the city, so they wouldn't go there. Instead they made their way up some side streets and in behind peeling, faded buildings suffering from long exposure to the humidity and rains of Kolkata, to the sort of slums that Dominique Lapierre's Hasari Pal was familiar with. Rani seemed to know quite a number of people there, including the Biswas family with their five children aged between one and nine. Judy sat on a small stool while Rani talked to the mother about a programme of pre-school education that she was involved in, aiming to help children like the Biswas children have a basis from which they might be helped to move forward to proper schooling. Rani said that it was quite a struggle at times to convince families to get involved, particularly when it came to girls.

Back at her hotel that evening, Judy had a shower and changed, but she couldn't quite shake off the noises and smells and images of the day. She sent a text to Kate – *in city up 2 neck. wow!* She dreamt that night of following Rani through endless alleyways, picking her way across dirty piles of rubbish and across foetid pools of dark green water while Rani kept on turning towards her with an encouraging smile. In the end the smile got too much for her and Judy suddenly burst out with a really aggressive shout – 'What are you smiling at? Stop it!'

She woke up at that point, fighting to free herself from the tangle of the sheet. She was sweating profusely and since the sensation of the dream was still with her, she found herself feeling guilty at having shouted at Rani in that way. After all, Rani had been so gentle and kind that day. So composed. So serene. So . . . Judy searched within herself for a word that would sum up the impression that Rani had made on her. So quietly *joyful* even – maybe that was it. As she thought of that word she had a picture of Rani moving in and out amid all the squalor of these slums with a genuine smile on her face. And to think that Rani and Ashish had been doing what Rani did that day for nearly three years – incredible. Looking at her watch she saw that it was just coming up to 3 a.m. and on an impulse she decided to text Kate – it would still be early evening back home. So off went the cryptic text – *Nightmare in city of u must b jokn joy*.

Judy's 'bookitis' was still with her, and she picked up another book, this time in Rani and Ashish's house. Somebody like herself, she presumed, had left the book there after a previous visit. It was a kind of 'thought for the day' book, with quotations from a whole variety of writers. Actually, this was not quite Judy's type of book, but when she picked it up her eye was caught by one or two striking stories and quotations that interested her. As she sat waiting for Rani to sort out some domestic issues before they went out again on another of her visits, Judy read one or two pages.

Always one for exotic, out-of-the-ordinary things or experiences, she was fascinated to read that when the French philosopher and writer Blaise Pascal died in 1662, they found that he had stitched a scrap of paper with some writing on it into the inside lining of his coat. He had apparently carried this bit of paper with him for the last eight years of his life. The words on that scrap of paper were very religious, but then he was a child of his times as much as I am of mine today, Judy thought, so she read on:

Fire: God of Abraham, God of Isaac, God of Jacob, not of the philosophers and scholars. Certainty. Certainty. Feeling. Joy. Peace.

It was a strange quotation and Judy didn't quite understand it, except that Pascal obviously found belief in God to be a certainty in life and that this gave him a sense of joy and peace. It was a far cry from her own philosophy of life at that moment, although she suspected that if she asked Rani what she thought, she might get a Pascal-like reply. Maybe she would do just that - ask Rani, who at that point had finished whatever she was doing and was now ready to go out. But asking deep philosophical questions as you stepped out into the crowded streets of Kolkata and had another go at negotiating the pavement obstacle course wasn't very practical, so the question wasn't asked. Instead, Judy concentrated on keeping close to Rani, who seemed to glide through the confusion of the streets with remarkable ease and grace.

They visited the Biswas family again and everything was fine. No immediate crisis, apart from the daily routine of living off a meagre income and having enough to eat and remain healthy. Near the end of Rani's round of visits, they met up with a couple of the volunteers that Judy had met at Rani and Ashish's house, and Judy smiled to herself when she saw that one of them was her blond Swedish giant. She noted that somehow in the context of where they were and what they were doing, the temptation to flirt and try out a bit of her considerable seducing powers had left her. Maybe this is what happens to you as you approach thirty, she mused to herself, but really she knew that being with Rani and having her eyes opened to the reality of Kolkata had flagged up for her an agenda of living that was quite different from the one she had been following up to then. So not even a return to Rani's house with Rani and the two volunteers stirred up anything more than a bit of pleasure from chit-chat on the way with people who were learning about Kolkata and its culture, even as she was.

That night, this time at a more respectable hour than 3 a.m., she sent an update text to Kate: *Came across Pascal tday, impressed.* That will get Kate going, Judy thought, and she was right. Kate got the text when she was at work and groaned out loud, which had a colleague asking her if she was all right.

'I'm fine,' she replied, 'but I'm not so sure about my friend Judy who is in Kolkata at the moment. I think she's an unredeemable serial killer.'

Naturally, this remark needed some explanation, but Kate's work colleague just laughed when Kate described Judy to her. 'Maybe this Pascal fellow will sort her out,' she said.

'Maybe,' replied Kate, 'but I doubt it.'

Back in her hotel room in Kolkata, Judy sat thinking about Pascal. Did he often fumble in the lining of his coat to fee where the scrap of paper was, she wondered? He must have had lots of doubts about things – doubts even about God or why else would he want to write a memo to himself and stuff it into the lining of his coat? This line of thinking got her wondering about the certainties that she had in her life, with the somewhat unsettling conclusion that she didn't have too many. A look in the mirror assured her that she still had her good looks and shapely figure, but was that the beginning of a wrinkle on her forehead? Surely not. But yes, there it was. She did a fast-forward thirty-year projection of herself and tried to imagine what she would look like then. There prob-ably wouldn't be much there to attract blond Swedish giants, she concluded. Ah well, that's life, she sighed. Better make the most of what I have now before it's too late. But then, what would it be like at sixty, to look back and see nothing much more than a jumble of fleeting experiences that had no real connection between them other than . . . well, other than what? That was the question. 'It would be really nice if I could have something of Pascal's certainty about things,' she said to herself, but he belonged to another age, I suppose.'

Rani said that Judy ought to see a bit more of India than just Delhi and Kolkata. If there were enough holiday days left she would like Judy to accompany her on a visit to her family. Judy did have time for that and she accepted the invitation eagerly. To be quite honest, Kolkata and its slums were beginning to get her down a bit. Maybe, like the TV clips of disasters in Africa, there was only so much you could take. Not everyone, after all, was cut out to be a Rani or an Ashish. So a couple of days after her first encounter with Pascal, she and Rani boarded a train at Kolkata's Howrah railway station, having picked their way through crowds of people sitting everywhere in the station forecourt as though it was some great urban

29

picnic. It was great to be with Rani, who pointed out all sorts of things that Judy would have missed if she had gone on the journey on her own.

It was an eight-hour train journey, so they had plenty of time to chat and doze and read and chat again. Rani told Judy about her family and how she and Ashish had met, while Judy did her best to fill Rani in with details about her life.

'Not quite so noble as yours, I'm afraid,' she said to Rani, who smiled and said that her life wasn't at all noble.

'But you and Ashish seem to be so contented in what you are doing, despite all the setbacks that you have from time to time. I wouldn't last a month doing what you do.'

'Well maybe,' replied Rani and she told Judy that she hadn't always been so contented. 'An elderly man I know was a great help to me. I think you'll meet him when you are with my family. Maybe he'll help you, because he is a very wise man.'

'That would be nice,' Judy said and they left it at that for the moment.

Judy was given a very warm welcome by Rani's family, even to the extent of having a 'welcome garland' hung around her neck. The family seemed to be well-enough off. Rani's father was a teacher in a nearby teacher training college and her mother was a nurse in the state hospital. Not quite the same as the Biswas family in Kolkata, Judy observed, but these sort of differences exist back home too, she reminded herself.

Unfortunately, not long after arriving at Rani's family home Judy began to get stomach pains. That could mean only one thing – she must have eaten something really bad before leaving Kolkata. The family was very understanding and sympathetic and she was told not to worry, but simply to rest and make sure that she drank enough clean water, with a little salt and sugar added to it. It was a miserable twenty-four hours, best left undescribed, before she was able to emerge rather shakily from her room into the living area of the house. Rani had been her ministering angel, something that made Judy feel very apologetic.

'You came here to see your family and get a rest from all this caring for other people. You didn't come home to end up nursing me.'

Rani just laughed and said that it was her pleasure. 'Fortunately the problem seems to have been something you ate at your hotel or in a restaurant and not in my house or even here in my parents' house. Anyway, it gave me the joy of looking after you.'

And there it was again – the joy thing. It seemed to be something that Rani had as a permanent companion, not looked for feverishly but travelling along with her into Kolkata's slums, along the cluttered streets, resident in her home when domestic crises arose, on board trains, and now while looking after a sick and vomiting foreigner whom she hardly knew.

Once Judy was up and about again, she enjoyed exploring the area around Rani's family home. She was able to text Kate in a positive way: *Stomach played up now OK w Rani at parent home Orissa fun++*. She followed up with an immediate second text – *Pascal still in pursuit*. The first text had Kate scrambling for an atlas to find out where Orissa was and discovering that it was an Indian state to the south of Kolkata. The second text left her confused. Who was this Pascal man? It must be serious if he was following Judy all the way from Kolkata to Orissa.

Rani's father said that before Judy left, she ought to get some fresh sea air into her lungs and the whole family had a delightful day on a lovely beach within relatively near reach of where they lived. It wasn't too crowded and Judy managed to find a place where she could buy one or two little mementos for her own family and friends back home. She got a little filigree silver pendant for Kate with an engraving of the blue jay on it, the Orissa State national bird. Kate deserved something nice, Judy thought to herself, especially after all those teasing texts from her.

It was on their return from the beach that Judy met up with Rani's 'wise old man'. Apparently he lived quite nearby. To Judy's surprise he turned out to be an Indian clergyman, of all things. She had been expecting some guru sitting in the dust with a mop of wild hair and a cloth wrapped Gandhi-like around him. She certainly didn't expect to meet this polite, refined elderly man, sitting at ease in a comfortable chair opposite her, engaging her in light and amusing conversation.

He didn't look like a clergyman, dressed as he was in a traditional dhoti (so at least he was one step in the direction of her imaginary guru) but that was what he had been for many years. He was quite small in build, with sharp eyes that studied her very carefully as he spoke. His command of English startled Judy slightly. There was no reason to think that an educated Indian couldn't speak English well, but his words were all so carefully chosen and precise. He was obviously highly articulate and after they had been conversing for a while it didn't come as too much of a surprise to Judy to learn that he had spent some years studying at Oxford University. He was of the age when to study at Oxford or Cambridge had been the pinnacle of academic achievement for many leading Indians in all walks of life. It wasn't quite the same now of course, Judy reminded herself, as she thought of India's rapid rise to being one of the world's leading nations, despite places like the slums of Kolkata.

As they sat eating some sweetmeats and spicy nuts that Rani's mother had brought to them, the conversation rolled along pleasantly. Judy had been bracing herself for some cryptic little phrases packed with meaning that she would need to chew over later to understand what they meant. After all, wasn't that what an Indian 'wise man' would do, steeped as he would be in the centuries' old tradition of Indian philosophy and meditation? But it didn't turn out like that at all. Instead, this little man kept the conversation bowling along at great pace with lots of little laughs and approving Indian-style sideways jerks of his head, as Judy told him why she had come to India and what she had made of it so far.

He sighed a little as she told him about her visits to the Biswas family in Kolkata, and sucked in his lips as she described her reaction to the squalor that she saw. He chortled over the story of the crow having a moving meal on the hunk of meat on the man's back, and he beamed with pleasure when she spoke of her admiration for Rani and Ashish and what they were doing. He seemed to draw everything out of her so easily and in such an encouraging way, stopping to ask her appropriate little questions which showed that he was really interested in her. The thought did cross her mind that maybe this was his old man's way of flirting with her – she was used to men who seemed to make her the centre of their attention for reasons that had more to do with her looks than for her, herself. But she dismissed that thought fairly quickly, telling herself that she knew genuineness when she met it.

Without really meaning to, she began to tell him that she was unsure how things were going to pan out in her life once she got back home. This visit had been great, but it had been unsettling at the same time.

'So what are you really looking for?' he asked her.

Without even stopping to think, she replied, 'What I want is to be sure of things and happy.'

Then she told him about the book she had picked up in Rani's house and the story about the message Pascal had written to himself, and sewn into the lining of his coat, and of how she half-envied Pascal's certainty about things and the joy and peace he seemed to find as a result.

'But I'm afraid I'm not very religious,' she said. 'Things are different nowadays from the time when Pascal was living.'

Having said that, Judy suddenly remembered that this alert, polite little man opposite her in his Indian dhoti was a clergyman. She had added quickly in an apologetic voice, 'Well, anyway, that's how I see it.'

It turned out that Rani's 'wise man' knew quite a lot about Pascal, unsurprisingly given his Oxford education. At the same time it still struck Judy as one of the eccentricities of life that she had had to come to India to learn from an elderly Indian gentleman about one of Europe's great gifted thinkers.

What followed fascinated her, because in his quiet, slightly squeaky, sing-song sort of voice, her new friend gave her more details about Pascal's life, and particularly about why he had written that message to himself.

'The story is that there was an accident at a bridge over the Seine around the end of November 1653. Pascal and some friends were travelling in a carriage that was crossing the bridge when the horses must have got frightened and panicked. They leapt or fell over the bridge, dragging the carriage with them. It came to rest on the bridge's parapet, leaning out dangerously over the water. Pascal and his friends managed to get out safely, but Pascal was quite overcome by the near-death experience and promptly fainted. Apparently he remained in a semi-conscious state for about two weeks – he was a very sensitive and nervous man it seems. He came to properly around 10.30 p.m. one night with the words that you read, burning in his mind like a fire. He immediately wrote them down on a piece of paper and sewed them into the lining of his coat, as you know already. That anyway is the story, and although some people doubt that the

"Memorial", as it is called, was written at that point, I like to think that it was.'

Judy thought it was a great story. She could picture the whole scene quite vividly in her mind.

'So, from that night on,' she said, 'Pascal was sure about everything, was that it?'

The answer to that question was held back a little by the arrival of some friends of Rani's who had heard that she was back home and had come to see her. So the conversation switched to talk about families and local news, in a mixture of English and Oriya. In the main, Judy just sat there as a spectator while the conversation flowed around her and her elderly clergyman conversationalist joined in that flow with an amused twinkle in his eye. After a while, he rose to take his leave.

'I'm so sorry we didn't manage to complete our little discussion about Pascal,' he said, 'but from what I have read, I don't think that he always found it easy to be so certain about things as he hoped. Having said that, his life was never the same again and thanks to that change we don't just remember Pascal today because he was a celebrated mathematician, but because he wrote these marvellous reflections of his – *Les Pensées*. At times, everybody needs a jolt in life to get things straight, don't you think?'

With further smiles to everybody, he was gone. Judy realised that, in the end, she had been given the parting gift of a wise saying – the sort of thing that she had half anticipated receiving from an Indian guru.

Rani had arranged for them to return to Kolkata on the overnight train, but before setting off Judy sent a quick text to Kate to keep her informed: *Lev 4 Kkata tonite w Rani think ++ Pascal.* Kate began to wonder if Judy would be back home at the end of her holidays or not. How long would this latest infatuation last, before the excitement and thrill dried up?

The journey back to Kolkata dragged a bit. Judy found it diffi-cult to sleep. The train seemed to be forever stopping and starting as it meandered its way northwards. She lost count of the number of half-empty stations she stared out at, with their sellers of fruit and snacks and tea moving up and down the platform beside the train calling on passengers to buy from them. Eventually the train pulled in to the general chaos of Howrah station and she and Rani managed to get a taxi to take them back to Rani's house.

As soon as they got out of the taxi, they knew that some-thing was wrong. You could feel it in the air and they didn't have to wait long to find out what had happened. The girl who helped Rani look after the volunteers came running out at the sound of the taxi. It was Ashish – he had been involved in an accident as he was setting out on his motorbike to visit a man who had promised to help them with a modest building project that they hoped to launch. A truck hadn't seen him on its inside and Ashish had been knocked over. He was now in hospital. The girl didn't know much else, since the accident had happened not all that long before Rani and Judy arrived in the taxi.

It turned out to be a long day. Judy didn't want to be in the way, but at the same time she didn't feel she could abandon Rani. Rani said that she would be very grateful if Judy could attend to one or two things for her, while she went to the hospital, so Judy stayed around for most of the day at Rani's home, before returning to her hotel.

The accident had been a bad one, leaving Ashish with a broken leg and a severe fracture of the skull. He had to be operated on that day to relieve pressure on his brain. By the time Rani got to the hospital – an excellent one not too fa away with a good neurology department – they had taken the decision to operate. Ashish recognised Rani, although he was very confused and not able to talk very well. She was told that there was no point in waiting at the hospital, but that she could phone and find out how Ashish was after he had had the operation. They said not to worry and that everything would be all right – 'How bland can medics get?' thought Judy when Rani told her this. But Rani had just smiled, even although anxiety lurked there in her eyes. She said she was sure they were right. It was amazing how calm Rani seemed to be. Judy knew that if she had been in the same situation she would have been tearing the walls down by now. Perhaps Rani was just being composed and fatalistic in an Asian sort of way that accepted accidents and tragedies as the inevitable in life.

But what moved Judy more than anything else was the number of people who came around to the house to enquire about Ashish and to support Rani. Four of the Biswas family arrived, bringing some mangoes as a 'thinking about you' present. Rani had no problems in accepting it, even although she knew how poverty-stricken the family was. She said later that it was a joy to receive the gift and that she was sure it had been a joy for the Biswas family to give it to her.

Ashish came through the operation successfully. Once he was back in the hospital ward, Rani sat with him for most of the remainder of the day. Towards late afternoon there was nothing more Judy could do, so she returned to her hotel, leaving a scribbled note for Rani to read when she came back home from the hospital.

Hope Ashish has a good night. Thinking of you. Will contact you tomorrow. I don't know how you can remain so calm.

37

Needless to say, Judy had not had much time to think about Pascal during the day, but as she flopped onto her bed, exhausted after the strain of the day and the effect of a more or less sleepless night on the train, she couldn't help wondering if the calmness Rani showed didn't have something to do with the stillness at the centre of her life. 'Maybe she's got a 'Memorial' sewn into her sari,' she thought, as she dropped off to sleep. Her dreams were a jumble of railway station crowds and doctors looming over her to tell her that there was little they could do for her, until Rani appeared to banish them with her smile.

In the morning she remembered to send a text to Kate – *Rani's husband accident but wil b OK Pascal on backburner*. Kate was sorry to hear about the accident, but relieved that Pascal appeared to be dropping out of things.

Judy was due to fly back home in three days' time. There was not much she could do the day after the accident, other than to phone Rani and ask her how Ashish was and to offer her help if Rani needed it. Rani thanked her, but said that she was getting lots of help – people were so good – so Judy ought to make the most of seeing some of Kolkata's more attractive sights. 'It's not all slums and poverty' she added. Ashish had had a reasonably good night and Rani was sure that he would be delighted to see Judy before she returned home. 'Tomorrow afternoon? Would that be convenient?' Judy said that would be excellent.

This left a day to fill in somehow. She could have gone on an organised tour of the city arranged by her hotel, but frankly she didn't feel up to it. Instead, she decided to go on her own and visit the Victoria Memorial Museum – a splendid domed and turreted colonial building standing in its own green space in Kolkata. There was an exhibition on in a section of the museum, under the title of Exploring India, recounting the travels of a certain Emily Eden to India in the late 1830s and displaying over seventy of her paintings and drawings. Judy looked at them with interest and wondered, if she were an artist, what she would draw or paint about the India that she had experienced. It would have to be a picture of Rani, she decided. She would have Rani standing at the door of the Biswas family home, looking in at the bare, essential furnishings of the house and greeting one of the children with a smile. 'Yes, she'll have to be smiling,' Judy said to herself. As an extra secret touch that only she, the artist, would understand, Judy decided she would have one of Rani's hands holding onto the waist of her sari where she kept her 'Memorial'. She laughed out loud as she thought about this, causing two Kolkata ladies nearby to look at her with surprise and alarm. Judy fancied she could see their thoughts appearing like a bubble out of their heads – 'Such odd people visit India these days, don't you think?'

Judy went to see Ashish the next day. He was pleased to see her and assured her that he was going to be all right after his 'near-death' experience. When he used these words, Judy's mind flashed back to the middle of the seventeenth century, with Pascal crawling out of his precariously balanced carriage on that bridge over the Seine.

'God was with me,' said Ashish. 'I must have something else to do for him.'

There was no point in asking why other victims of street accidents didn't survive and where was God when these happened – typical of me to be so cynical, Judy thought to herself. Instead she smiled and said, 'Of course, I'm sure you're right.' Rani, who was there, smiled at her when she said that. Everybody seemed to be smiling. It was getting quite infectious.

That night she sent her last text to Kate – *See u soon bringing Pascal and Joy home with me*. Kate blinked when she read that.

39

She wondered if Pascal and Joy were married, or partners, or just friends. She thought it was just like Judy to leap into a friendship like that and end up bringing both these people back home with her. 'But that's Judy for you,' she thought, as she went round to Judy's flat to turn the heating on, in order to give Judy a bit of welcoming 'Kolkata warmth' as she stepped into her house. She noticed that Dominique Lapierre's book *The City of Joy* was still lying on a small coffee table where Judy had left it.

'She must have forgotten that,' she said to herself.

The Eyes Have It

The future is long, the past is short;
love of peace gives a wide space;
love of evil gives a narrow place

Karen saying

In the castle of my soul there is a little postern gate,
Where, when I enter, I am in the presence of God

Walter Rauschenbusch

He walked with a limp and used a stick for balance. It wasn't that he was all that old, far from it, but his poorly mended broken ankle was playing up again. Not surprising really, when you think of all the days of walking he had just done. The couple of weeks trudging across forest-covered hills – and they were steep in many places – not to mention fording innumerable streams and small rivers, would have tested out two good legs, let alone one good leg and a distinctly dodgy second one. That second leg was looking quite a mess. The skin had broken around the bad mend on the ankle and the open wound was showing the yellow signs of infection. It needed expert attention before things got worse.

Cha Ker Paw was probably in his mid to late 40s. He was a big, powerful-looking man with one of those faces that a nineteenth-century novelist would have described as 'noble'. His hair was thinning on top, his broad forehead continuing up towards the crown of his head, while the rest of the hair lay all around in a thick ring of waves and curls. His face was set off by a surprisingly luxuriant beard. I say 'surprisingly' because it wasn't common among his people to have such a big beard.

The beard contributed significantly to the 'nobility' of his face and so far it sported very few grey hairs. His eyes were the dark brown eyes of all his people, except that in Cha Ker Paw's case they seemed to be especially dark and brown and . . . well what? To be a bit over the top I would say that if some Hollywood producer had been looking for a 'Jesus face' for his blockbuster movie, Cha Ker Paw would have been his man. There was an aura of something special about him, despite the messy open wound at his ankle which had you looking away quickly. But once you had looked away, you seemed to be drawn back to look at his face every time. You couldn't stop yourself from focusing in on those eyes. They were so still, and at peace.

Now I don't know much about eyes, apart from recognising that some are brown, some green, some blue and some red (after too hard a night). But there are times when you see a pair of eyes and say to yourself, 'That person's been through a lot.' It's not the colour, of course, but it's what seems to come out of the eyes and across to you as you look at them. A window into the inside of the person, I suppose. That's hardly an original thought, but it does. As I said, I'm not an expert on eyes. Anyway, when you met Cha Ker Paw you knew that his eyes hadn't just been handed down to him by his parents or bought ready-made over the counter. They were eyes that he had won. This story is about the winning of those eyes.

But first there is the problem of the wound on his ankle to sort out. Cha Ker Paw pointed out, very reasonably, that to go to a hospital would be a risky business for him. It wasn't that he doubted the skills of the medical staff to help him, but he was in the country illegally – 'Yet again,' he said, with a little twisted smile. This was bound to come out and then what?

But here I am, rattling on, and you don't even know the setting of the story, although the 'forest-covered hills' and the name 'Cha Ker Paw' are a bit of a give-away. If I say that Cha Ker Paw is a Karen from Burma and that, as he swithers about going to hospital, he is in a neighbouring country to Burma, will that do for you? No point in saying too much.

But back to Cha Ker Paw and his ankle. There are times when you know that no amount of arguing and reasoning is going to change the way a person thinks. This was how it was with Cha Ker Paw and his need to go to a hospital. After a time, you just have to give up. The arguments peter out and you are left with the rock-like stance of someone who is not going to budge. 'Thank you, but no thank you,' was the sum of his response. When last seen he was limping off back towards the hills and to who knows what lay ahead.

Out of sight, of course, did not mean out of mind. His face or his ankle? It was hard to determine which memory was the stronger of the two. It had been his ankle that had been looked at and discussed and 'tutted' over – it really did look nasty – but it was his face and his eyes that carved out for themselves the deeper memory in the minds of those he had left behind.

So who was he, this Cha Ker Paw with his noble face and memorable eyes, who limped off and left us, and whose wounded ankle threatened to bring his life to an end? It took some time to put the story together, since Cha Ker Paw had left little snip-bits of his history with people here and there. It was like the pieces of a jigsaw that had to be collected first and then laid out in traditional style – the flat edges first and the more colourful inner picture later. With this jigsaw, unfortunately, there was no picture to follow or use as a check, since the picture had walked off into the hills.

The 'edges', so to speak, were fairly easily put together. I asked around and most folk seemed to know the rough outline of his life. Some folks thought they were related distantly to him, so they told me, but no one could be classed as close family.

'Does he have any close family?' I asked.

'Probably not,' was the answer, 'at least not now.'

'Why, what happened?'

'The usual – killed or died because of the troubles. He's not the only one to have had that happen to his family.' This was something that I had heard on other occasions and it was always said in a fatalistic way, as though this was the unwelcome, but inevitable, outcome for some in the Karen/Burmese struggle.

It turned out to be almost impossible to track down what had happened to make him lose his family, but one rather wizened old lady put some facts together in between puffs on her pipe. She said that she knew the village where Cha Ker Paw had been born. 'I used to go there from time to time. It was over there in the direction of the great river.'

As she said this she waved her hand in a vague westerly direction out towards Burma.

'But the village isn't there any longer. It was burnt down by the soldiers.'

'And the villagers?' I asked. 'What happened to them?'

She thought about that for a moment, took another puff of her pipe, set her lips up for a very proficient spit to the side away from me, and then shrugged her shoulders.

'Who knows? Dead maybe or in the forest, or perhaps in a refugee camp somewhere.'

But someone else was certain that Cha Ker Paw's parents had been killed. He was sure he had heard that. In any case, if his parents were still alive, Cha Ker Paw would have referred to them surely, but during his visit he had said nothing. I had to be content with that.

The other bits of his life's outline that I managed to put together, were that at some point Cha Ker Paw had been a soldier, fighting for the Karens against the Burmese.

'Didn't you see his tattoo?' a man asked me.

'No.'

'Well he had one all over his chest. I saw it when he was washing.'

'What kind of tattoo?'

'A lion or at least the outline of a lion. That's the sort of thing a soldier would have. Something to make him brave and courageous and to be feared.'

I tried to imagine Cha Ker Paw as a soldier. He had the physique for it, I thought, but could those eyes of his ever have squinted through the sights of a gun at another man and sent a message to his finger to pull the trigger? I couldn't see that picture clearly. As I was trying to take this image of Cha Ker Paw on board, the other man had gone on talking. He was of the opinion, although he couldn't be too sure, that Cha Ker Paw had been someone important in the armed struggle, but that had been a few years back, he added. Recently, Cha Ker Paw appeared to have done nothing else but wander from place to place.

'Did he tell you the places he had come through in the these two weeks of walking?' he asked me.

'No,' I replied.

'Well, they were really dangerous places. That man's not scared. I wouldn't have done what he did, I can tell you. He's a really tough man, that's what he is.'

'Tough?' I said. 'Yes, I suppose he is, walking all that way with his ankle in that condition, but on the other hand he seemed a gentle kind of man, didn't he?'

'Now, maybe, but you can bet that he was a hard, frightening sort of man at one point.'

This last thing was said by a man who had just joined the group where I was sitting. I looked at him and classed him as 'tough' himself. I asked him if he knew Cha Ker Paw and all he would reply was 'Maybe.' Not a very satisfactory answer, but he didn't have the look of a man who would welcome supplementary questions, so I had to leave it at that. Annoying really, but there was nothing else I could do. All I could hope was that I would have the opportunity to speak to this man later, but he moved away from our group immediately after having spoken. I asked someone if they could tell me his name and was told that it was Thoo Hray. I wrote that down in my notebook, so as not to forget it. You'll gather that by now I was getting quite fired up in this quest to find out more about Cha Ker Paw.

Later that night as I lay in bed and thought about things, I did what all good detectives do – or at least as they do in detective novels and films – I reviewed what I already knew about Cha Ker Paw. At least I had something to work on – born in a village in Burma somewhere near a big river; his village burnt and destroyed by the Burmese Army; his parents both killed maybe – but did he have any brothers and sisters? A soldier, and maybe an important one at that, in the Karen fight against the Burmese; and then, a broken ankle at some point – but how did that happen? And finally this wandering in dangerous places, carrying about with him an air of mystery and what I could only describe as 'peace'.

The day after Cha Ker Paw had limped off into the hills again and I had had these question-and-answer conversations with people, I was up at dawn with the rest of my neighbours. I was standing outside in the early morning sunshine ladling water out of a pitcher and washing myself, when I caught sight of Thoo Hray just a short distance away. He was standing with his back to me facing the hills, obviously hard at it brushing his teeth as he brought his morning wash to an end. He gave one last spit into the grass and turned round. He couldn't help but see me. From where I was, it seemed to me that he paused for a moment as though deciding what to do, then he turned and walked off towards the house where he had been sleeping.

'I hope he's not going to take to the hills like Cha Ker Paw before I've had the chance to speak with him,' I said to myself.

But that is exactly what he did, much to my frustration.

When I had finished my washing I had gone along to the house where he had been sleeping, meaning to fix up a time when we could meet and talk, only to be told that he had gone already.

The whole thing might well have gone on to join the many unknowns about people around me, if it hadn't been for a chance meeting with Thoo Hray a few months later. I had stopped off at a little eating place that I sometimes frequented when passing that way – they had a nice noodle dish that I was partial to – and who should be sitting there at one of the tables but Thoo Hray. He recognised me immediately – not too difficult a task really – but more to the point, I recognised him. We greeted each other politely and he made no objection to my suggestion that I should share his table space. We were the only customers at that moment, something I was glad to notice since I felt that our conversation would flow more easily if there was no one eavesdropping. And so it was that I learned more about Cha Ker Paw, as well as about Thoo Hray himself. The one seemed to set off the other, with frequent switches from the background cloth to the central jewel in the box and then back again to background cloth, as their stories unfolded. Because what I discovered was that their lives had been very closely intertwined. Very closely indeed.

If the overall impression coming from Cha Ker Paw's eyes had been one of peacefulness, then it was more or less the opposite that I got from Thoo Hray's as I sat opposite him eating my noodles. His eyes were restless and even angry looking, which made it a bit daunting to try and initiate a conversation with him. But taking my courage in both hands I raised the subject of Cha Ker Paw, after we had exchanged the normal innocuous chatter that is part and parcel of a casual encounter. He seemed to be expecting it in any case, presumably from the moment that he saw me entering the eating house.

'Since we last met on that brief occasion a few months ago, I've not been able to get that man Cha Ker Paw's face out of my mind,' I said.

He made no reply to that, but by the way his lips spread out and down from the corners of his mouth just for a moment, he seemed to be saying to me, with a bit of sardonic resignation, 'Well, good for you. Join the club,' or something like that.

'You don't happen to know,' I continued, 'if he ever got that ankle seen to? He really ought to have gone to a hospital. But, of course, I realise that that would've been difficult. Still . . .'

'No, I don't know, but he'll be all right. He always is.'

As he said that, Thoo Hray gave a brief snort and jerk of the head. I wondered if that was going to be that as far as talk about Cha Ker Paw was concerned. I didn't feel that I could push it any further. However, to my relief he went on. 'I've known Cha Ker Paw since I was a boy.'

I knew then that I was going to get the story I was waiting for.

It came out slowly, and there were times when I wondered if my source was going to dry up, because it was obvious that Thoo Hray had mixed feelings towards Cha Ker Paw. At one moment he was almost hero worshipping him and then he would switch to speaking about him with frustration and annoyance, even tinges of anger. It was when these latter feelings were dominant that I feared Thoo Hray would stop speaking altogether, so I was careful not to have any eye contact with him at that point. Any hint from me that I was siding with Cha Ker Paw against him would have been bound to ignite these smouldering dark eyes and shut the door into the past that, despite himself, Thoo Hray was opening up for me.

There was about five years' age difference between them, so Thoo Hray informed me, which meant that Cha Ker Paw

49

must have been about thirteen years old when the Burmese destroyed his village. Thoo Hray remembered the occasion vividly enough, although not the actual destruction of the village. He had been with his mother collecting betel nuts from a plantation of trees that they owned some distance from the village. They had knocked down quite a number of nuts, and were getting ready to carry them back home, when three neighbours of theirs had arrived in a panic to tell them the Burmese soldiers had arrived. It was just about then that they heard gunfire in the distance and they knew that they would all have to flee deeper into the forest up towards the hills. It was a strange sort of day, Thoo Hray said, because walking through the forest seemed such a normal thing to be doing. Nothing had changed in their surroundings. The only thing that had changed was in the atmosphere of fear that hung over their little group. Even the eight-year-old Thoo Hray could sense that. Everyone seemed to know that there would be no going back to the village, even although it was only later that day that they found out what had happened to it.

They decided to stop and set up a rough camp at a place that they knew well, near a stream – by this time they had been joined by some others and now there were about twenty of them there, including children. It was far enough away from the village to be out of danger from the soldiers, but not so far away that they couldn't find out what had happened to their homes and the other villagers, once the soldiers had gone. Late that afternoon Cha Ker Paw joined them. You could see from his face that something terrible had happened. Maybe he had been crying, but by this time the tears had gone, or at least Thoo Hray couldn't remember seeing any. What he did remember was Cha Ker Paw standing there surrounded by others and with a face twitching in contortions saying, 'I'll kill them . . . I'll kill them . . . I'LL KILL THEM ALL . . . I hate them . . . I HATE THEM.'

It was some time before he quietened down.

'Maybe he cried then,' said Thoo Hray to me, 'but I'll never forget that shout of his. I think we all knew that's what he would do and I thought it was great. He was so angry. It was magnificent.' As he said this, Thoo Hray clenched his fist, bringing it hard down on the table and almost knocking over the bottle of water in front of him.

Some others had trickled in to join their group, who were able to confirm and add to what Cha Ker Paw had told them. The Burmese soldiers had arrived suddenly, so suddenly indeed that not everyone had been able to escape. They rounded up the people who had not been able to flee, picking out the men. Cha Ker Paw's father was in that group. They then searched the houses and when they had done that, set fire to them. They said the village had been helping to support Karen guerrilla fighters. They took four of the men, including Cha Ker Paw's father, and shot them in front of everybody else, at which there was a sudden dash for the surrounding forest by the remaining villagers. The soldiers opened fire – these must have been the gunshots Thoo Hray and his mother had heard earlier. Cha Ker Paw got separated from his mother and his young sister and brother in the general melee and dash for the forest. He had spent most of the day since then hunting for them, going back as near to the village as he dared, but without having any success. From a distance he had seen the soldiers moving about the village, burning the houses, and he had seen them carrying bodies and flinging them into the flames. He had come to the conclusion that all his family had been killed, although people tried to reassure him by saying that his mother and sister and brother were probably hiding out somewhere else in the forest and that he would find them in a few days once the immediate crisis was over.

Thoo Hray told me that they must have waited in their temporary forest camp for two or three days. The Burmese soldiers made no attempt to sweep the area for surviving villagers. So, a few days later, some people were able to go back to the village to see what had happened. All the houses had been destroyed and in the still-smouldering embers, they discovered some badly charred, unrecognisable bodies. They must have buried these bodies, but Thoo Hray couldn't remember anything about that.

He had not gone back to the village, but had journeyed on with his mother to a Karen safe place, where they hoped that Thoo Hray's Karen-soldier father would meet up with them once news of the destruction of their village had got to him. After a few days, Cha Ker Paw himself eventually came to join them, after spending more futile time in the vicinity of the destroyed village searching for his mother and sister and brother. His father, of course, was one of the dead, as everyone knew. Cha Ker Paw was convinced by now that his whole family was dead.

'I was younger than he was,' said Thoo Hray, 'so he didn't pay too much attention to me, but whenever I saw him, he seemed to be on his own. He never smiled. That was the thing you noticed about him, he never laughed and he never smiled.'

I was tempted to suggest to Thoo Hray that he never seemed to smile himself, but for obvious reasons I didn't dare risk that sort of comment at this stage in the story. Nevertheless it was interesting, I thought, that Thoo Hray should pick out that particular memory of Cha Ker Paw. When, I wondered, did Cha Ker Paw begin smiling again, and when did Thoo Hray stop?

Just then, Thoo Hray paused and stood up. A vehicle had pulled up outside the eating house and it looked as though we were going to have company. I turned round and saw that i was a police car. Thoo Hray didn't panic or anything like that, but with a quick movement he picked up his cloth shoulder bag in which, I suspected, he carried his betel nuts, chewing leaves and paste, and said that he would need to go. And then he said a surprising thing.

'Having started to tell you about Cha Ker Paw, I want to finish the story.'

He told me that, if I wanted, I could make my way back up the road in the direction from which I had come, until I came to a single large tree at the left-hand side of the road, about half a kilometre away and just beside a house set back a few yards from the road itself. He would be there to meet me. In the meantime, he said to me with the hint of a smile of sorts, he would leave me to the company of the policemen. With that he slipped out of the back entrance of the eating house, just as a couple of policemen entered. They sat down at another table and began a very loud conversation with each other. They gave a nod in my direction and I returned the informal greeting, hoping that they wouldn't wonder why there were two plates and two glasses on my table and only one person sitting there. But they seemed to be in off-duty mood and not at all interested in me or my table. After a respectable lapse of time, I got up and went out.

I found the tree and the house without any bother. Thoo Hray was there already, sitting in the shade of a small veranda at the entrance to the house. He got up to welcome me and invited me to sit down on a somewhat battered-looking canvas chair alongside where he had been sitting. A young woman appeared and brought us two glasses of water. Thoo Hray introduced her to me as one of his extended family – a cousin or a second-cousin's daughter, I didn't quite catch what he said. He seemed to be at his ease, but the girl was less so. She shot him glances with reserve and more than a little apprehension in them. She seemed to be slightly afraid of him. I could understand that, because as he sat there he was a formidable brooding presence, with his powerful body and arms, stern face and those dark, angry-looking eyes. Not the sort of person you would want for your opponent or enemy, I thought.

Thoo Hray picked up the story from where he had left off in the eating house. He said that, at that time, there were still some Karen strongholds that had not been subdued by the Burmese and it was to one of these that Thoo Hray and his mother went. Cha Ker Paw was there with them briefly before going off on his own again one day. They presumed he had made his way to another of the strongholds a bit further to the north of them. It must have been about six years later, Thoo Hray thought, that he next saw Cha Ker Paw.

'It was the fighting season again. The monsoon season was over and everybody knew that the Burmese Army would be on the move once more. There was talk of a great military sweep against the remaining Karen strong points and everyone was tensed up. Preparations were being made for defending the place where we were and more Karen soldiers had arrived to help. Among them was Cha Ker Paw.'

By now Thoo Hray was old enough to be able to help in some of these preparations. Even at fourteen years old he was big and strong, he said of himself, and at times he found himself working alongside Cha Ker Paw. When it got really hot and sticky, Cha Ker Paw would take off his shirt, exposing the lion tattoo on his chest and greatly impressing the younger Thoo Hray in the process. It strengthened his own resolve to be a soldier like his father and Cha Ker Paw, and so be able to fight the Burmese Army that had destroyed his village. Remembering Cha Ker Paw's vow on the afternoon that his family had been massacred, Thoo Hray asked Cha Ker Paw one day if he had ever killed a Burmese soldier and so begun to get his revenge. He never got a direct reply. Cha Ker Paw just bent down to attack another obstructing root with his machete, but the way that he hit the root with real force and venom said it all. Thoo Hray wondered how many of the enemy had been at the receiving end of that same force and venom. The viciousness of the machete blow, and what it implied, stayed on in Thoo Hray's mind with a lot more effect than would have been the case if Cha Ker Paw merely had replied boastfully with a 'four' or 'five' or 'six'.

The big attack didn't materialise that year, apparently, although Thoo Hray said that everything was kept at a level of high alert and most of the Karen soldiers stayed around. Some, however, were sent on special operations – it was common knowledge. Inevitably, it seemed, Cha Ker Paw was among this chosen elite and once again Thoo Hray lost touch with him. Tales filtered back all the same, of some of the daring raids that were made. It was heady stuff, even allowing for the morale-boosting exaggeration of what had been achieved. With half a million or more soldiers at its disposal, the Burmese regime was never going to be defeated – not even by Karen hit-and-run sabotage groups like the one Cha Ker Paw was on. But it made good story-telling in the evening, after the main rice meal of the day was over and the betel nut was being chewed and spat out and conversation had become more expansive. Cha Ker Paw's name kept on cropping up more frequently as one of the most daring members of these sabotage groups.

'When did you become a soldier then?' I asked Thoo Hray. I was beginning to worry about my time and could see myself sitting there on that veranda all day as Thoo Hray went into every detail of what had happened. A quick short-cut to later on in the story was needed, I thought.

Thoo Hray looked at me and I could see annoyance in his

eyes at being interrupted in this way. Apparently he was not a man who like to be crossed, even in a small way.

'Me?' he said. 'Oh, that was later.'

'And did you ever go along with Cha Ker Paw on his special missions?'

Thoo Hray frowned and looked at me suspiciously. 'Why do you ask?' he said.

'Well, just because of the way things work out in life, it seems likely that coming from the same village you would join up together at some point.'

Thoo Hray paused and I could see him making up his mind whether or not to continue. I wondered if I had blown it and began to wish I hadn't interrupted him. After all, who was I, as far as Thoo Hray was concerned? Maybe I would meet and say things to people that I shouldn't say and word would get to the 'hunters' of people like Thoo Hray. The incident in the eating house had alerted me to his fugitive status. He took a long look at me and this time I knew that I would have to hold his gaze. I succeeded and thankfully Thoo Hray relaxed a little.

'All right then,' he said with a firm nod of his head. 'I did become a soldier and I did fight alongside Cha Ker Paw. He was our leader by then and he was the one who taught me how to kill people.'

He said that with an air of real defiance, challenging me to take it on board and see what it did to my obvious admiration of Cha Ker Paw. I had enough sense not to make any reply and so Thoo Hray went on talking.

Without giving any details of time or place, or indeed much in any way about what had happened, Thoo Hray told me that he and Cha Ker Paw, along with others, had been engaged in a fire fight with a group of Burmese soldiers. It had been an ambush of some sort and in the end the Burmese soldiers had fought their way through, but not without casualties on both sides. It was only a matter of time before Burmese reinforcements would arrive to clear the area, so the Karen attackers withdrew fairly quickly into the forested hills. It was as they were just about to leave that Cha Ker Paw and Thoo Hray came across two badly wounded Burmese soldiers in the bushes near to where the ambush had taken place. They looked in bad shape and were moaning. They asked for help and said that they were in the Burmese Army only because they had been forced to join and not because they wanted to harm the Karen people. Cha Ker Paw had stood for a moment looking at them, then turning to Thoo Hray he said that the only way to deal with people like these was to kill them. He did this with his machete, rather than alarm others by firing a gun or wasting a couple of precious bullets.

'So what do you think of that?' Thoo Hray said to me with a sneer on his face.

'Not very pleasant,' I replied. 'But I doubt if Cha Ker Paw is doing that sort of thing today.'

Thoo Hray turned his head away from me and spat. If you could get venom into spittle, then that spit had it. I almost expected to see it sizzle on the dusty ground in front of us.

'You're right. He isn't.'

It didn't need any explanation. 'Going soft' was something despicable and obviously a betrayal to the cause, in Thoo Hray's mind.

'So what happened?' I added. Another bold move by me in the conversation, but I wanted to find out more.

I suppose Thoo Hray knew he was going to tell me more, but he wanted to pause, either to sort out in his mind what he would tell me or maybe just, like a good storyteller, to heighten the tension. So he unhooked the cloth shoulder bag from the back of his chair and produced a clear plastic bag with some betel nuts in it. I had been right about the bag. He offered some to me, but I declined and just sat watching him as he cut the nut, smeared one of the leaves taken from another bag with the red paste which he kept in a little tin, laid the betel nut on the leaf, rolled it up and popped the lot into his mouth. It wasn't long before he was ready to launch his first blood-red spit to join the other dark stains on the ground around the house. Wiping his lips but still chewing, he resumed talking, spitting from time to time. Maybe the spitting helped him with what, for him, was the distasteful part of the story.

The rot, in Thoo Hray's interpretation of things, had set in one evening back in their forest camp. By now, the Karen soldiers had been reduced to a forest guerrilla army. Their fortified strongholds had gone. A concerted assault by the Burmese Army during one of the previous dry seasons had seen the end of these strongholds and of any more pitched battles – even defensive ones. It was in one of the many scattered soldiers' camps, then, that Cha Ker Paw and Thoo Hray and their companions found themselves sitting around a low fire one evening discussing tactics. Morale was not too high, despite some recent moderately successful hit-and-run attacks. Still, there was no thought of giving up their fifty-year struggle against Burmese domination. The clearing out and burning of villages by the Burmese, along with the injustices of forced labour, continued to fuel the resolution of the Karen soldiers and stiffened their determination to keep on fighting.

Not for the first time, talk had veered round to discussing what they would do when victory was finally theirs to enjoy. There was the sharing of some idyllic dreams about what life would be like, but then they began to speak about 'getting justice' and revenge for many of the things that had happened. There were more than just Cha Ker Paw and Thoo Hray there who had seen their villages destroyed and members of their family killed. One or two began to go over again some of the revenge which they had already extracted and they described vividly what had happened. Thoo Hray had joined in that. The stories got more and more lurid – or exaggerated – but it was noticeable that Cha Ker Paw, who was their commander, had kept silent. They asked him what he thought, but he preferred to say nothing, although he didn't stop the others from going on with their stories. He seemed to be taking a step back from everyone else all the same and that, according to Thoo Hray, was the first sign of the 'rot' that had crept into him.

They did more raids from time to time, and Cha Ker Paw was just as resourceful, courageous and daring as ever. An excellent commander. But you could see it in his eyes that he wasn't getting the same kick out of it all as previously.

I was listening intently to all this, but the mention of Cha Ker Paw's eyes – the first time Thoo Hray had referred to them since he began telling me the story – made me sit up. Now we are getting to the heart of things, I thought to myself.

It was about a couple of months after that evening around the camp fire, Thoo Hray said, that he and Cha Ker Paw were together again on a mission. By now they were a recognised and formidable pairing and tended to operate up front of the others. The ambush that had been prepared went off at half cock and they all had to get away from the scene in a hurry. It was more or less every man for himself for a bit, as they made their way to their pre-arranged rendezvous point and Thoo Hray lost contact with Cha Ker Paw. Once at the meeting point, Cha Ker Paw was conspicuous by his absence. Dangerous though it was, there was no hesitation about going back to look for him. Thoo Hray and two others were the ones who went. Things had quietened down and once again the Burmese soldiers had opted not to follow their attackers too far into the forest, until there were more of them to do so in reasonable safety.

'I came upon Cha Ker Paw very quickly,' Thoo Hray said. 'This was very fortunate for him, since I hate to think what the Burmese soldiers would have done to him, especially if they had found out who he was.'

'So what had happened?' I asked.

'He had been wounded. His ankle was all smashed up.'

'Ah! That ankle,' I said.

'Yes, that ankle,' replied Thoo Hray. 'He was in great pain and unable to walk or even do much crawling – not that that would have got him very far.' He stopped at that point and with a distasteful twist to his face said, 'He wasn't on his own.'

I waited for an explanation, being careful to avoid eye contact with Thoo Hray – I was getting quite expert at judging these tricky moments. After a moment, he continued. The other person there had been a badly wounded Burmese soldier. Thoo Hray never found out how it came about that the Burmese soldier and Cha Ker Paw had got together, but somehow they had. Maybe Cha Ker Paw had done a bit of crawling after all. Both of them still had their guns, which lay on the ground beside them. This struck Thoo Hray as very odd, since all he knew of Cha Ker Paw would have suggested that by now the Burmese soldier should have been dead.

The knowledge that the Burmese might still be somewhere in the neighbourhood was the only thing that stopped Thoo Hray or one of the others from shooting the Burmese soldier immediately. It would have to be a knife or machete job again. Quiet, over in a moment and then carry Cha Ker Paw back to safety as quickly as possible. Cha Ker Paw knew the drill. After all, he had been their instructor.

The first thing they had done was to snatch up the Burmese soldier's gun. No point in running risks, even although the

Burmese soldier appeared to be only half conscious. The next thing should have been his quick despatch and that would have happened if Cha Ker Paw had not intervened. 'No! Not that!' It says something for the respect they had for their commander, that in the heat of the moment, with all the urgent need to get away as speedily as possible and with adrenalin running high, they obeyed that command. There had been a moment when things seemed to freeze. Thoo Hray had turned to look at Cha Ker Paw and object to the command, but had been caught by the resolute look in Cha Ker Paw's eyes.

I intervened smartly at that point. The reference to Cha Ker Paw's eyes prompted me. 'Say that again,' I said, 'the bit about his eyes.'

But this time Thoo Hray wouldn't oblige by giving any explanation, unless the really angry look from him and another blood-red, betel-nut-induced spit was his answer.

When he was ready to go on with the story – I didn't dare repeat my request – Thoo Hray said he had hoisted Cha Ker Paw to his feet and helped to drape his arms around the shoulders of his companions. But before they left, Cha Ker Paw had insisted that they make the Burmese soldier a bit more comfortable and leave some water with him. He was bound to be found fairly soon once the Burmese began their concerted sweep of the area, Cha Ker Paw had said, and the story he would tell of having had his life spared would say a lot more than his dead body would ever communicate. It was only the high esteem that Thoo Hray had for Cha Ker Paw and the discipline of their command structure that stopped Thoo Hray, who was following behind to cover their retreat, from making an excuse to go back to the scene and do to the wounded Burmese soldier what he felt should have been done in the first place. It was clear that in Thoo Hray's reading of things, the 'rot' in Cha Ker Paw was now out in the open and dangerously undermining his resolve. It perplexed him and made him raging angry at the same time, since the courage and ability of Cha Ker Paw as a soldier were never in question. For Thoo Hray it needed leaders like Cha Ker Paw to remain hard and resolute, if they were going to have any success against the Burmese.

As it happened, Cha Ker Paw never again took part in any attack against the Burmese Army. Part of this, of course, was due to his injury. Thoo Hray told me that once they had got back to safety Cha Ker Paw did receive some medical attention, but as I had seen for myself the ankle never did mend properly and he had had constant problems with it ever since. But there was more to it than that. Something else of some significance must have happened.

Just as we got to this part of Cha Ker Paw's story, there happened one of those extremely frustrating incidents which, I suppose, any investigative writer or journalist has to get used to. A man appeared from the house, and introduced himself to me as a cousin of Thoo Hray's, presumably the father of the girl who had brought us water at the start of our conversation. He said something to Thoo Hray in a language I didn't understand. Thoo Hray raised his eyebrows a little and shrugged his shoulders.

'I'm sorry,' he said to me, 'but I must be off. As you might have gathered, I need to live my life on the move.'

I said I understood, but I had been hoping to hear more about what had happened to Cha Ker Paw.

'I'm sure you'll find someone else to tell you about that,' Thoo Hray said. 'Our ways have really parted since then.'

'But you did see him those few months ago when we first met?'

Thoo Hray looked at me with another of those quick angry looks I had got used to. 'Not a successful meeting that.'

With that he rose up, unhitched his cloth bag from the back of the chair, said goodbye quite formally, went into the house and, I presume, made another backdoor exit to somewhere else a bit more secure.

There was nothing else to do but to take my own leave, having thanked Thoo Hray's cousin for the hospitality of his veranda. Before setting off to walk back up to the road, however, I made the comment, 'Your cousin Thoo Hray is a very formidable and impressive man. But tell me, does he ever really smile and laugh? He seems so tense, with things pent up inside him.'

'That's Thoo Hray. He's been like that for years. I don't suppose he'll ever change,' the man replied.

'His friend Cha Ker Paw changed all the same, from what I have learned. Did you know him?'

It was worth asking the question, although I didn't think I would get a positive answer, and I didn't. So with some more polite farewells, I left.

Having heard so much about Cha Ker Paw and Thoo Hray and what they had done in the past, I didn't feel at liberty to go around asking people if they knew them. So I had to abandon the story and content myself with imagining what else might have happened to Cha Ker Paw. However, this story might never have been written had it not been for another strange twist in events.

I happened to be up very early one morning, when I saw three large vehicles parked outside a row of local authority buildings. The vehicles were only partially covered with tarpaulin and so I could see that they were packed with people. I knew instantly who these people were and where they were going. They were illegal immigrants who were on their way to the Burmese border where they would be dumped in a refugee camp that actually straddled the border. The hope was that they would not return – a vain hope, in many cases, because people who had nowhere to go ahead of them might as well risk all the problems of turning back over the border. I stood looking at the vehicles for a moment or two. There was nothing I could do about it. It was when I was standing staring that I saw Thoo Hray. He did not look well. In fact, he looked distinctly unwell. So he has been caught, I thought, and I wondered if who he was and what he had done had come out in the detention camp interrogation.

I don't know whether or not he saw me. Perhaps he did, but if so he gave no indication. I walked on, so as not to draw too much attention to myself and shortly after that the vehicles moved off on their way to where they would dump their human cargo. I knew instantly what I was going to do. I would try and get permission to go to the refugee camp on the border and see if I could track down Thoo Hray, both to see how he was and also to seize the opportunity of finishing the Cha Ker Paw story.

It took me about a week to get the permission I sought. Once at the refugee camp I made discreet enquiries and found myself eventually in the bamboo-constructed camp hospital. Thoo Hray was there, lying on a bed in a remarkably clean and airy ward. He had been there since he arrived, I was told. If the ward seemed peaceful enough, that wasn't the case with Thoo Hray. He seemed restless and agitated.

'I've got to get out of here,' he said after we had greeted each other. 'It's just that I'm so weak. I can hardly stand, far less walk. Changed days for me.'

This last comment was made with a return of the old flash of anger in his eyes. They hadn't changed, I noted. I didn't like to ask too much, but I gathered he'd had a hard time in the detention centre after he had been picked up and his weak ened body had succumbed to some fever or infection. I gave him some oranges I had brought with me and that seemed to please him. At least he was in better condition than the six or seven men sitting on the floor of the veranda outside the ward. They stared into space, still traumatised by their experiences in the detention centre.

Just as I was wondering how to introduce the subject of Cha Ker Paw, he got there ahead of me. 'So now, I suppose, you can hear the end of the Cha Ker Paw story. That's why you've tracked me down here, isn't it?'

I said, 'Not entirely,' but he didn't appear to pay any attention to my reply. He seemed lost in thought. I knew better than to try and interrupt him.

It took quite a time for Cha Ker Paw's ankle to mend sufficiently for him to be able to get around, Thoo Hray told me, but they didn't see much of each other, since Thoo Hray was soon back on 'front line duties'. It was the second or third time that they met after the incident when Cha Ker Paw got his injury – Thoo Hray couldn't remember precisely the sequence of events – that Cha Ker Paw made it clear he had had a big shift in his thinking and attitudes.

'He told me that he had had a dream,' Thoo Hray said.

'What kind of dream?' I asked.

'One about his parents and family.'

Thoo Hray couldn't remember all the details, but it had something to do with Cha Ker Paw finding himself back at his destroyed and burnt-out village. The houses were in ruins, with smoke still rising from the charred remains. Cha Ker Paw was looking for the bodies of his parents in the blackened heap that had been his house, when his parents and his brother and sister suddenly appeared standing before him. A great surge of joy ran through him and he was just about to step forward and greet them, when he found that between him and them lay a pile of bodies. Some of them had been shot, while others had blood still flowing from knife wounds. With a start, he recognised that they were all Burmese soldiers. His mother had one arm round Cha Ker Paw's little sister and was pointing to the bodies with her free hand. She was crying.

There was more to the dream than that, but apparently it was this image of his mother pointing to the bodies and crying which came as a jolt to Cha Ker Paw. Was she crying because of what these Burmese soldiers had done to her and her family when they were alive, or because she was pitying them lying there in such a sordid heap?

'But when he told me the dream,' said Thoo Hray, 'I knew which way his mind was working. That day when he had looked at me with such determination in his eyes and said, "No! Not that!" He had given up by then. He was finished.'

Thoo Hray was too weak to indicate his contempt and anger with a violent gesture of any sort, but his eyes blazed. I could see that the drifting apart from each other, which had begun earlier, had become an acknowledged open rift between them once Cha Ker Paw had shared his dream and his thoughts on it with Thoo Hray.

'Yes, I suppose you're right. It must all have been working in his mind,' I said after a moment's pause to let Thoo Hray calm down. 'Is that not how Cha Ker Paw saw it himself?'

'No. He said that God had given him the dream. He said something about a bright light shining behind his parents and he knew that that was God.'

'And what do you think?' I asked.

Thoo Hray gave me one of those sardonic, slightly twisted smiles of his. 'That God told me to kill Burmese soldiers and clear them out of our land.'

I didn't feel that I wanted to pursue this line of things too much, so I let his remark pass and went on to ask him what

Cha Ker Paw had been doing since giving up being a soldier. Thoo Hray said that as far as he knew Cha Ker Paw had devoted his time to visiting Karen groups hiding in the forest. He would take things to them and just spend time living with them. His reputation ensured that he always had a welcome and people listened carefully to him when he spoke to them.

'What did he talk about?' I asked.

I wondered if Thoo Hray would reply to this question, especially since he was now out of sympathy with Cha Ker Paw's view of things, but he told me that Cha Ker Paw talked about his past and about doing things in a different way and, of course, he talked about God. He was always talking about God, apparently, and about his dream and the inner peace that he said he now enjoyed. When people asked him why he continued to risk his life by doing all this wandering about in dangerous places, his favourite reply – one he had given to Thoo Hray at their last meeting – was to quote from a Psalm in the Bible that said God would look after 'his going out and his coming in, this day forth and for ever.'

'So that was that then, was it, between Cha Ker Paw and you?' I said at length.

'More or less. But I keep meeting him at odd times and in odd places.'

'Does he try to argue with you and make you change your mind?'

'No, but he has the annoying habit of smiling and telling me that he understands my outlook.'

'You don't like that?

'*No, I don't.*'

As I looked down at a weakened and thinner Thoo Hray lying on the bed, catching his eye as I was doing so, I couldn't help but compare him with the injured, limping Cha Ker Paw. With Thoo Hray there was a such a restlessness and suppressed rage, while my brief memories of Cha Ker Paw were of the calmness and inner contentment that shone through his eyes. Now I knew, or could guess, how it was that he had won these eyes for himself and I felt that my quest had come to an end. There's a story in this, I said to myself. Yes, quite definitely, there's a story here to be told, and that's what you've got in front of you now, to make of it as you will.

There is one final little twist, all the same, which might interest and intrigue you. It certainly left me wondering. After taking my leave of Thoo Hray and thanking him for telling me Cha Ker Paw's story I left the refugee camp. I stopped at the military post at the outskirts of the camp to have my papers checked and was just about to resume my journey when I took one last look back. My mind was filled with the pathetic image of Thoo Hray lying on his bed and I was wondering what would happen to him, when I saw a person walking away from me in the direction of the camp hospital. It was a man. A big man who was walking with a stick and limping. I couldn't go back through the military post to check, but I am almost certain it was Cha Ker Paw on his way to see Thoo Hray.

I spent the rest of the journey home imagining what they would say to each other and what would be the outcome of their meeting.

The Long Hard Journey

Whereby a man doth not only bear adversities, injuries, reproaches, and such-like, but also with patience waiteth for the amendment of those which have done him wrong.

Martin Luther

You could see the boat coming while it was still some distance away. To start with it was not much more than a white smudge on the horizon, but as you watched, the smudge began to take on the shape of a boat. Of course, the sun and shimmer of heat hovering over the river tended to play tricks with your eyes, but if you were someone like Mbile you had long since got accustomed to that and you knew when a boat was a boat. In any case, you knew where to look for it – downstream just to the left of the nearest island, before it disappeared behind some other islands. In thirty minutes or so it would be here and the general pandemonium of arrival would begin. Noise, shouting, laughter, jostling, pushing out of canoes in haste to get to the boat first and make a quick sale – Mbile had seen and done that a hundred times or more. But today was different, because 'he' was coming. That had been Mbile's first thought when he woke that morning after an uneasy night's sleep. You never could tell when the boat would arrive, so you tended to sleep with one ear open for the boat sounds – the deep throb of the engines or the sudden blast of the siren as the boat drew near. It would be a disaster if he didn't get there in time to greet Ntoko as he came off the boat.

It was hardly light when Mbile emerged from his house that morning and splashed some water on his face. It didn't seem so long ago that he would have noticed Nselibeka had been up before him and gone off in the dark to her 'garden' along with her neighbours, cashing in on the cool hours of the day to do what had to be done there. On a boat day she would probably have spent the night with her friends down by the river waiting for the boat to come – her canoe laden with bananas and mangoes, cassava roots and leaves. But Nselibeka had died two years previously. A fever – malaria, presumably. Mbile still missed her acutely. She was the bright one. Lots of ideas about things. Always smiling. Could sing really well too. The marriage had been more or less arranged between their families, but he had been lucky and had liked her from the start. Ntoko had arrived and everything was great until they learned that Nselibeka was not going to be able to have any more children. Some people thought he would end the marriage and get another wife, or at least keep another woman on the side, but that was not the way Mbile saw things.

'Ntoko is just fine for us,' he would say, and people would reply quickly – maybe a bit too quickly, 'Of course he is.'

There wasn't a great deal to do in the early morning once he had let the chickens out, apart from sometimes boiling water for a mug of tea, but he didn't always do even that. He was known for living very simply and there were few luxuries in his life. A mug of tea was a borderline case. Anyway, since Nselibeka's death there was less money around. It hadn't been easy before then, but it had certainly become more difficult since. She had always been one for thinking up ways of getting a little extra income and now that she was gone . . . Still, he did earn something regularly and for that he was grateful and then there was always a little fishing that could be done. Ntoko had to be thought of all the time.

Every month he went to one of the local traders and gave him some money. It wasn't much, but it was something. It was a matter of trust that the trader wouldn't cheat him, but so far it seemed to have worked. Ntoko had been able to go to the trader's brother in the city and get that money minus some-thing for 'handling expenses', as the local trader put it. This had helped to ensure that Ntoko had a little extra – there were so many things you needed to get in the city, he had written to his father, and Mbile could well believe that. Nselibeka's brother had done the proper family thing and agreed to help in seeing Ntoko through his secondary school education, but there were limits to what he could do. He had six children of his own, after all. So Mbile's monthly arrangement with the trader was still needed.

From early on it had been obvious that Ntoko was a bright boy. As he grew older, he began to look more and more like Mbile. He had the same strong body, well muscled and lean, and although his eyes were not quite the same as Mbile's, the shape of his head was. If he had become a grass-cutter and part-time fisherman like his father, he could have done that well. But it was clear that Ntoko was destined for greater things. He had his mother's quick mind and interest in all sorts of things and he had shone at primary school.

'This boy needs to go to secondary school,' they were told. 'Our country will need clever people like him in the future. The sky's the limit for him, you know – such a clever boy.'

So, after a lot of family discussion, Ntoko had gone off to a school in the city. Nselibeka's brother had said that it was like a gamble. If it came off, then they would all benefit if Ntoko 'made it' in the city. Mbile couldn't quite come to accepting that approach, even although it might be true. What he wanted was the best thing for Ntoko and, as he watched the chickens scratching around outside his house on the morning Ntoko was to arrive by boat, he wished it even more. If only Nselibeka had been here to welcome Ntoko back home and see him with his State Diploma at the end of his six years at secondary school in the city. Mbile pursed his lips and frowned slightly. She would probably have had the welcome home meal organised by now, he thought, while all he knew was that he was going to kill one of his chickens later on and there wouldn't be much more than that.

By now the sun had begun to come up and a loud clanging rang out from nearby. Mbile went back into his house, reached up to the rafters and took down a plastic bag that had been stuck up there under the roof. In the bag was a battered-looking red hymn book and a Bible. Closing the door behind him, he made his way through his neighbour's yard to a little mud and thatch building. Outside the building there were a couple of poles from which was suspended a metal bar that a man was beating with another metal bar. An improvised 'church bell'. It seemed to do the trick, all the same, and soon there were about twenty people gathered in the little chapel. They sang a hymn, listened to a bit of the Bible being read, and prayed. The singing was slow and almost plaintive: *O God, our God, we thank You for your mercy shown to us all.* No Nselibeka, thought Mbile, but Ntoko is there and I am going to be seeing him today. His face beamed as he sang and his voice sounded out strongly as he was caught up in the comforting slow rise and fall of the singing. It was his turn to pray and his prayer was full of confidence. People could feel it – rescue from the threats of the night; wonder at a new day; delight in the goodness of God.

'His son's coming today,' people said to each other and they smiled, because they liked Mbile.

Back home, he had something to eat. There was a neighbour who made a very nice sort of fried dough ball and Mbile was very fond of them. He tore off a bit of dried fish and ate that along with one of his cassava/tapioca puddings that served as his staple food. His water came from a spring down by the river so it was clean, although some people doubted it, claiming that it was bound to be fouled. But Mbile had a strong constitution and he was rarely ill.

Time to leave the house. He looked down at his shirt. It wasn't his best one. He reserved that for Sundays when it was his turn to help out at the big Communion Service held in the main church. Three or four hundred people could be there and you were very much in the public eye on these occasions. People would look oddly at him if he met the boat wearing the Sunday shirt. That left just the shirt he was wearing and another one that he would need to wash at some point that day. As he glanced down, he saw that the left shoulder was a bit torn. Maybe the shirt's days were nearly over, but he had seen bigger tears than that in his shirts, so this was nothing new. He gave the shirt a reassuring tug, as well as a sort of ritual rub to a dark stain just below the collar – it had been there for weeks. Anyway, Ntoko was not going to be interested in his shirt.

Mbile had managed to get the day off from his grass-cutting, so he was free to make his way down to the beach in front of the shops. That was where the boat usually put in, if the water level wasn't too low. He would just wait there until it did. He was good at waiting. He had lots to think about in any case – Ntoko's arrival; what he would be like; how they would greet each other; what they would talk about; what Ntoko's mother would have felt – well, maybe not too much of that. No point in opening old wounds. There would be others there waiting along with him. Some would be there to sell things to the boat in the way Nselibeka used to. Others would be hoping to go upriver on the boat, and they would be surrounded with boxes and bundles and exude an air of importance that all travellers seem to have – we're going somewhere, while you just stay on here. There would be people like him, waiting to welcome a family member or a friend coming home from the big city. Waiting would be full of interest, watching others and smiling from time to time as he confirmed that his son would be arriving that day.

74

'Did well at school, I hear.'

'Yes, got his diploma.'

'You must be very pleased.'

'I am.'

As he sat at the beach, standing up every now and then to check if the boat was in sight, he thought of Ntoko. He could see him as a baby. Nselibeka was so proud to go out and about with him wrapped closely to her back. She was a good mother and Mbile had felt so strong and fulfilled as he watched the baby feeding at his mother's breast. My child. Our child. Then came Ntoko's first tottering steps towards exploring the world around him. He seemed to learn so fast. Incredible. Are all children like him? He took to reading and writing as though it was already part of him inside and it only needed an opening to get out into the world.

'He'll go far,' they said many times.

Sometimes Ntoko would hear them and say, 'I will. I will.'

When he had gone off to school in the city he had been so excited. 'I'll come back, you know. I'll come back when I am an important man in the Government.' And although he laughed when he said it, you knew that he meant what he said.

Ntoko had been back several times since then during the school holidays, but not since Nselibeka's death. He wasn't there for the funeral – Nselibeka had died so quickly. She just lay there in the morning asleep . . . except that she wasn't asleep. They buried her that afternoon. Ntoko had arrived two days later. The house was full of relatives, and Mbile and Ntoko didn't say much to each other. Mbile wanted to say something, but Ntoko seemed to stare him out every time and the words wouldn't come.

Mbile got up at that point and took another peer down-river. He didn't like to think of a silent Ntoko not speaking to him. Nselibeka had been the more outgoing of the two of them and she and Ntoko would often laugh together over something that had happened or over something someone had said. He never quite managed that sort of easy banter with Ntoko. Even before Ntoko went off to school in the city, Mbile had noticed that he was less inclined than before to come fishing with him or to help him in any way.

'Just growing up, I suppose,' Mbile had decided. 'And you can't draw any conclusions from the unusual time just after his mother's death.'

As he stood there looking downriver thinking all these thoughts, suddenly the boat appeared. The white smudge on the horizon was instantly recognisable. Ntoko would soon be here. The muscles of Mbile's arms and chest tightened involuntarily as he put a grip on the quiver of anticipation that came over him.

The trouble with the boat's arrival was that, after having seen it a long way off, you lost sight of it until it had almost arrived. A nearby island blocked the view. So you just had to wait and get everything ready. People would get into their canoes and shout across to each other in raucous, excited 'market voices', a pitch above their normal voices and several decibels louder. Two or three trucks would appear and a group of local policemen would take up positions on the river bank as a token contribution to law and order, occasionally stepping in when the confusion or arguments spilled over into something a bit too violent. Some soldiers from the military camp would arrive, toting their guns and looking around assertively at everybody from under their brown helmets. And all the time, people's eyes would be searching for the first glimpse of the white superstructure of the boat, as it slid along the far side of the island before rounding the point and coming in to full view.

When it did, everybody would swing into action. Canoes would push out from the river bank in a mad scramble to get to the boat first and tie up alongside it. Boxes and bundles, if not already in canoes, would be carried to the edge of the water. More people would arrive just to watch and share in all the bustle. The boat's siren would let out a long blast to announce its arrival in style, while its bow would edge its way slowly into shallower water. Sometimes, as happened this day, the water was deep enough for it to get within touching or plank distance from the small jetty, so making it easier for people to get on and off.

Mbile took up his position just beside the jetty, while his eyes scanned the length of the boat for any sign of Ntoko. At last he saw him making his way forward to the landing-plank. Mbile waved, but obviously Ntoko didn't see him, since there was no wave back. He seemed to be deep in conversation with some smartly dressed city types in their white shirts and city sunglasses. Ntoko too had sunglasses, but he had shoved them up on to his forehead, which is why Mbile recognised him. Mbile himself had never worn sunglasses, despite all the glare at times when out on the river fishing. Nselibeka had never had any either. Mbile smiled to himself at the almost surreal idea of Nselibeka coming back in her canoe from her down-river garden, sporting a pair of sunglasses. That would have provided gossip for a week or more among the neighbours.

He could see that Ntoko was wearing a smart white shirt like the others and that he appeared to be very much at ease with whoever these others were. They would probably be speaking in French. Mbile knew some French, but not much. He had never spoken it to Ntoko. He was very conscious that his pronunciation was poor and thickly accented. By now, Ntoko was getting nearer to the bow of the boat, so Mbile waved once more. But again there was no indication that Ntoko had seen him. He and his friends were laughing and gesticulating wildly at something. It must have been a good joke.

'Any sign of your son yet?' asked a man standing next to him.

'Yes, I can see him there with some friends. He's just coming up to the plank now, I think.'

'Is he going to be staying with you for long?'

'I don't know. He might. Depends on what he wants to do, I suppose.'

'A clever lad. He's done well.'

'All that came from his mother, I think,' said Mbile modestly, knowing that it was probably true all the same.

'One of these days he'll be arriving here in a helicopter as a really big shot,' the man said with a laugh, 'and you'll be rolling in money.'

Mbile screwed up his face and shook his head. 'No, I don't think so.' As he said that he had a flashback to the days of patiently teaching Ntoko the skills of fishing on the river. 'All the same, I'm sure he won't be a fisherman and grass cutter like me, not with all that education.'

There were four policeman preventing people from going onto the jetty itself, so Mbile couldn't go forward and greet Ntoko as he stepped off the plank. He would just have to wait that fraction of a second longer. After two years of separation, that could be endured. He looked at Ntoko and thought how much he had grown. A boy no longer. A man. Erect and broad-shouldered already. A father's pride. A mother's too, but then . . . Mbile gave his head a little jerk as though to banish that thought. In a moment, Ntoko would be back home. Mbile's face broke into a delighted welcoming smile.

Afterwards, he tried to work out what had actually happened. It seemed important to get it right. Ntoko was still laughing as he stepped off the plank, pretending to stumble as he did so and making his friends laugh again. It was as he was getting his balance back that he looked straight at Mbile standing behind one of the policemen. For an instant their eyes met and Mbile pushed forward against the policeman, ready to reach out his hands in welcome. Ntoko's eyes were blank. Not a flicker of recognition. The next moment he was off the jetty and halfway up the river bank, leaving Mbile standing in confusion behind him. It was Ntoko's voice, this time not in French, which had shouted out, 'Look at all these people. They're all here just to welcome us.'

There was more laughter. His group seemed to be in very high spirits and Mbile wondered if it was possible they had been drinking, even though it was still morning. He hoped not. But he was sure Ntoko had seen him. How could he make a mistake in recognising the face of his own father, even after two years? Maybe it had been a sort of joke, and the next moment Ntoko would turn round and come charging down the river bank, back to where Mbile had been left standing. But no, he hadn't even looked round. Instead, he walked on with his friends to one of the waiting trucks.

'I should have put on my best shirt,' Mbile muttered to himself, looking down at the tear on his left shoulder and giving another rub at the stain. 'I should have realised that he would want to arrive home looking his best and be met by his father looking his best too and not in this torn old shirt. If I had thought of it, I could have even borrowed a pair of sunglasses from someone. I'm sure he would have noticed me then and let his friends know who I was. I'll tell him that later and apologise.'

But even as he muttered all this to himself, he knew that it was nonsense. No son should ignore his father like that. He suppressed a feeling of real anger and annoyance.

'There's maybe some special reason that I don't know about yet. I can find that out later.'

He was brought out of this turmoil of thought by the voice of the man next to him. 'You've missed him. That was him wasn't it? Go on, get a move on before he thinks his father has forgotten to come and meet him.'

Mbile was genuinely startled by the sound of the man's voice. Time seemed to have stood still. He had become trapped in that one moment when Ntoko had looked at him without any recognition. He took a step forward, almost involuntarily, and got an angry dig in the ribs from the policeman who was trying to keep people back.

'Yes, he didn't see me,' Mbile said with a half laugh, 'it's all this crowd of people. Almost as bad as in the city.' With that he began to push his way past people and make his way up the bank behind Ntoko and his friends.

The question of what Ntoko was going to do was solved within a week. He got a job teaching in the newly established secondary school. His State Diploma didn't actually qualify him to teach, but there were few with even his level of qualification around and the new school snapped him up almost immediately. It was immensely satisfying for him to walk along the road and receive the acknowledgement of people. The pupils he taught in the new school were just about as proud as he was and gave the impression that they had arrived at university already – no longer pupils in a school, but students. This helped to boost Ntoko's standing by a few more notches in the eyes of others. His high status was backed up further by the solid fact that he was living in rather a nice house formerly used by a European teacher – three rooms, kitchen, inside bathroom and running water from the rainwater storage tank. A far cry from his boyhood home with Mbile and Nselibeka. The house went with the job as a way of ensuring that he didn't go off to the city again, as he had been tempted to do. He would go back there, of course, but in the meantime he was happy to mark time here.

Mbile was glad to have Ntoko nearby. He didn't see much of him, although Ntoko would sometimes appear at his house to see if his father had any fish. Mbile had asked him once if he wanted to borrow his canoe and go fishing for himself, but Ntoko had said that wasn't the sort of thing a secondary school teacher did. So Mbile always gave him some fish. No payment was asked for, or offered.

Mbile's monthly visits to the local trader with cash to forward to Ntoko in the big city stopped, only to be replaced by a greater expense as Ntoko made it clear to him that now that he was living in a big house there were certain essentials that he needed. It was remarkable what he seemed to need. Mbile thought it would have been much better if Ntoko had got installed in a simpler house, but he didn't like to say that directly to his face. So he would go to his tin box yet again and extract another few bank notes and hand them over.

'One day, I really will have lots of money and I'll not need to come to you for help,' Ntoko would say with an air of supreme confidence in his own future prospects.

Despite giving away money which he required for some of his own essentials in life, Mbile wasn't sure that he looked forward to the day when he would not be needed by Ntoko. The connection between them seemed to be fragile as it was. So maybe it was better to have little in the tin box and continuing contact with Ntoko, than a full box and no contact.

The memory of the day of Ntoko's arrival lingered on. It had been like a curtain coming down between them and this curtain had only been lifted slightly in the days that followed. The city friends who had come up on the boat with Ntoko didn't stay around for very long. After three days they went back downriver to the city. During these three days, Mbile saw very little of Ntoko. In fact it was only at night, late on the day of his arrival, that Ntoko had turned up at the house, walking into the yard as though he had been out for the day and this wasn't his first meeting with his father in two years.

There was no special meal. There could have been, if only Mbile had managed to have a word with Ntoko before he and his friends jumped into the back of the truck and drove off. But by the time Mbile came out of his stunned reverie and pushed his way up the river bank between people going to the boat and coming off the boat, it had been too late. So he just made his way home and hoped that Ntoko would get in touch before too long. He had recognised the truck as belonging to the local State Administrator – presumably Ntoko's friends had links with that family and would be staying there. It would only have added to his embarrassment and, presumably, to Ntoko's as well, if he had gone up to the Administrator's house and asked if his newly arrived son, whom he had missed welcoming off the boat, was there. There were always people milling around that house who would be only too glad to make gossip out of it. Mbile felt he could do without that.

He took the riverside path back to his house. No point in going up by the shops or along by the school and the big church, where he was likely to meet too many people he knew well. The boat wasn't long in getting under way again and he watched it go past, still with canoes tied to its sides like beads on a necklace, as buying and selling continued. One by one the canoes would untie themselves and with a flurry of frantic paddling to avoid the worst of the wash at the stern of the boat, would drop back – business done until the next boat arrived in a few days' time. Nselibeka had done that sort of thing on a weekly basis. Mbile wondered what she would have made of Ntoko's conduct that morning. Would she too have been ignored? He doubted it. They were so close. But he had been ignored. He began to feel angry again.

Of course, he did meet people on his way home. There were always folks on the move, either going to the river to wash their clothes or fetching water from one of the springs or carrying loads somewhere or walking to the shops and market.

'Where are you going?' they said to Mbile.

'To my house.'

'Did your son arrive on the boat then?'

'Oh yes. He's got some business to do at the moment. He'll be home later.'

'Is he well?'

'He's very well.'

'You must be so pleased to see him.'

'Yes, I am. I'm very pleased indeed,' Mbile replied to them all as he walked on hoping that the turmoil within him didn't show itself in either his face or voice.

Once he was back home, he fetched a coiled bunch of forest creepers from a corner of his house and took it and a small wooden stool outside, planting them both down under the shade of a tree in his yard. With his machete he began stripping the creepers and preparing them for use. From time to time he liked to make fishing baskets that girls and women used to catch fish in the shallow waters near the river bank. He got quite a good price for these baskets, so it was always worthwhile making them. Stripping the creepers was mechanical work and this suited Mbile, because while his hands were occupied in their very familiar task, his mind was free to think.

Mbile was a good man – that, at least, was his local reputation. He was not known for getting ruffled and aggressive in any way. He had the walk of a man in control of himself and no one questioned his integrity. When he stood up to pray, as he had done that morning in the little chapel beside his house, no one had any doubts about him. His devotion was genuine and coloured the whole of his life. Yet, on the day that Ntoko arrived by boat, Mbile sat there under the tree in his yard and he felt that he had an evil spirit sitting beside him as his companion. He was angry.

There were those around Mbile who would certainly have suspected that an evil spirit was at work, causing Ntoko to act in the way he did and Mbile to react angrily inside himself. 'You could get some strong, helpful medicine for that from you-know-who,' they would have said. But Mbile didn't even begin to think about going down that road. Instead, as his hands worked away expertly at their task, he prayed to God for help and under-standing. After a time he felt the anger and hurt go out of him and he was at peace. Ntoko was his only child and, come what may, he would always love him. So when Ntoko appeared that night, he was able to welcome him warmly and naturally.

'Ntoko, my son! It does me good to see you. I was at the boat today, but there was such a crowd there, that I think you didn't see me. I just hope you didn't think that I had forgotten to come and welcome you. Anyway, I knew that you would be busy with your friends, but you would come home later.'

Ntoko made a half-hearted attempt to show surprise that Mbile had been at the boat, and without looking his father straight in the eye, said, 'I never saw you. I had some friends that I've been with today and they must have blocked my view. There was such a crowd of people there. Anyway, I'm here now and I'm completely exhausted.'

'Have you eaten?' said Mbile. 'I was going to kill one of the chickens but I didn't know when . . .'

'I'm not hungry,' interrupted Ntoko and without saying much more to his father he dumped his bag inside the house, went to the pit-toilet in the yard, then turned in for the night. It wasn't quite the homecoming that Mbile had pictured.

While his friends from the city were around, Ntoko disappeared each day to be with them. Perhaps they asked him where his home was, but he never offered to bring them there on a visit, nor did he suggest to Mbile that he should come and be introduced to them. Conversations between Mbile and Ntoko were very matter of fact, either for a few moments in the morning before Ntoko took off for the day or briefly, late at night, when he returned home. Mbile hoped that it would be different when these friends had gone.

On the fourth day after his return home from the big city, Ntoko surprised his father by turning up for morning prayer at the little chapel beside their house. His friends had gone downriver the previous evening. Quite a fuss was made of him by the others at the chapel and Ntoko joined quite heartily in the singing. Mbile felt a burden slip from his shoulders and he smiled at everyone. This was more like it. He tried to put away the thought that maybe Ntoko had gone there merely to enjoy receiving the congratulations and adulation of others. I mustn't think like that, Mbile thought.

At just before seven in the morning it was still quite cool. A lovely time of the day. The sun was well up, but not too far up, and you could sit outside without having to retreat into the shade. Mbile and Ntoko sat together and, for the first time, had something approaching a proper conversation before Mbile headed off to work. Ntoko even asked his father how things were going with him and appeared to be making an effort to smooth over the hurt of the last few days. Mbile responded with warmth and asked in return how life in the city had been. Later that day, when evening had come, they were still able to chat together, although Mbile avoided any mention of what had happened a few days previously when the boat arrived. Ntoko kept off that subject too. It was almost as though they had made a secret pact with each other to avoid raising the issue. Things began to feel more normal again. Ntoko had lots to talk about and he had Mbile laughing at some of the things that had happened to him in the big city. At that point, Ntoko was still uncertain what he would do, but Mbile said that something would crop up. The main thing was that he was home.

'It's so good to see you,' said Mbile. 'I'm proud of you. You've done so well.'

To which Ntoko had the grace to give a sort of shuffling, half-embarrassed acknowledgement.

It was the following day that Ntoko was offered the job of a teacher in the secondary school. He didn't waste any time in replying. It was a matter of saying yes straightaway and, naturally, accepting the offer of a house to live in. This meant that Mbile and Ntoko ended up living apart and seeing each other only occasionally, as when Ntoko turned up looking for fish or for a little help from his father to make some essential purchase. The closeness that they had begun to enjoy on that fourth day of Ntoko's return seemed to dissipate as Ntoko got caught up in his new life of being a teacher. Their lives became parallel lives, with only rare moments of touching. Mbile was disappointed, but he was glad that there had been some moments of genuine closeness. Similar moments would surely come again – and they did, but hardly in the way that Mbile had expected.

The first inkling that there was a problem came when Mbile was at work. He had just got into the rhythm of swinging his grass cutter – a long, thin machete with a sharpened curve at the end – when a teacher from the secondary school came up to him. 'Do you know where Ntoko is?'

'No, I don't,' replied Mbile, lowering his grass cutter to rest on the ground beside him. 'Have you not tried his house? Or maybe he's gone to the market.'

But even as he said this, Mbile sensed that something was wrong. It's easy to catch the whiff of someone else's uneasiness. So he added quickly, 'There's nothing wrong is there?'

'Well that's the problem. We can't find him anywhere.'

Mbile said that he would go back to his house and see if Ntoko had left any message, although he thought that was unlikely. He was halfway home, when a boy came running up behind him and said that the headmaster of the school would like to see him urgently. Mbile turned round and retraced his steps to where he had been cutting grass quite near the school.

It was a very complicated story that the headmaster told him. News had just arrived that Ntoko had been put in prison in a place in the interior about a hundred miles away. It all had something to do with the setting up of a new school at that place, and Ntoko's decision to go there on his own and try to establish a rival school. This had led to a near riot and since Ntoko was seen to be the one who had started all the trouble, he had been arrested and put in prison.

'But why did he go there?' said Mbile as he tried to absorb this news, 'and how did he manage to get there in the first place?'

'He got a lift there on a motorbike a couple of days ago when the school was on holiday, but as to why he went there and tried to do what he did, that's something only Ntoko can tell us. He's a very confident young man, as you know, and he's not always . . . well, it doesn't matter at the moment,' added the headmaster looking at Mbile standing before him and seeing the concern in his eyes. 'This is something which we can sort out, I'm sure, but we will need to act quickly. In any case, we need our teacher back here, don't we?'

As he said that, the headmaster gave a sort of half-laugh to put Mbile at his ease. Mbile didn't feel inclined to share in the half-laugh, but he smiled and said, 'Of course.'

It was decided that the headmaster and a couple of others should set off immediately to the place where Ntoko was in prison and see what they could do to get him released. Mbile insisted that he should go along with them and he managed to get time off his work to do that. It took over five hours along rough roads to get to their destination, enough time for Mbile, sitting in the back of the truck, to think things over. This was one time when he was glad that Nselebeka wasn't alive. She would have been devastated to think of her son in prison.

It was nearly nightfall before their journey was over. People knew why they had come and there wasn't too much of a warm welcome given to them. Still, they were given a place for the night. Mbile made his way along to the prison to see if he could make contact with Ntoko and give him some food that he had brought with him. The prison was of the makeshift variety – nothing much more than two or three windowless brick huts with big wooden doors and a few ventilation holes spaced around the walls just below the roof. The policeman on duty said that he couldn't let the prisoner out, since it was now night and if he let him out he might run off into the dark. So all Mbile could do was to give him the food and hope that it would get to Ntoko.

'Tell him it's from his father and that things are going to be all right.'

The policeman took a look at the food, felt it and then sniffed it. 'Fish, is it?' he said.

'Yes.'

'Mm!'

The policeman said that Mbile could come back in the morning and see the prisoner then. Prisoner . . . prisoner. The word was like a knife cutting into Mbile.

As it happened, he didn't have to go back to the prison to

see Ntoko, because things moved forward in the night. It was agreed that first thing in the morning there would be an official hearing by the local Chief, who doubled up as the State Representative, and on whose orders Ntoko had been arrested and locked up. So there they all were in the cool of the early morning, seated in a circle outside the Chief's house, ready for the hearing to begin. The prisoner was sent for. This was certainly not how Mbile had pictured things working out for Ntoko. He felt sorry for him and yet, at the same time, annoyed. It isn't easy for a father to see his son as a prisoner.

Ntoko appeared barefoot between two policeman carrying rifles – was he really going to try and run away, thought Mbile? He looked dishevelled. His shirt was stained in several places and his trousers were rolled up to just under his knees. Not the perfect image of an educated secondary school teacher. The confident swagger of the Ntoko coming off the boat a few weeks previously had been replaced by a shamefaced shuffle.

He caught sight of his father immediately. Their eyes met and this time there was instant recognition before Ntoko dropped his eyes to stare at the ground. Mbile's heart skipped a beat. He should have been agonising about Ntoko's predicament, but instead he felt like singing, because in that brief glance he and Ntoko had found each other again. He was sure of that. All was going to be well.

The hearing got under way with due deference being made to the Chief by all who spoke, even to the point of clapping hands loudly three times before saying a word. It had all been a mistake. Youthful enthusiasm for education. Never any intention of setting up a rival school. Important that we all pull together for the better future of our young people. Promises of some help from the now successful secondary school where Ntoko was teaching, and so on. Mbile hardly listened. He kept on watching Ntoko who began to stand up a little taller now that he realised things were being worked out. It took some time, but eventually after a brief recess for the Chief to think things over, the policeman were told to step back and Ntoko was free to walk towards his group of liberators. Mbile reached out and gripped him by the shoulder, smiling broadly as he did so. What do you say in such circumstances when joy and embarrassment are so mixed up together? All Mbile could say as he smiled was, 'Did you get the fish I sent you last night?'

'Yes, some of it at least,' said Ntoko looking his father straight in the eyes and then adding, 'thanks for coming.'

For Mbile, that was enough.

They didn't waste any time in beginning their journey back home. They collected Ntoko's things, including his shoes which, as a free man, he could now put on, and set off. The headmaster said nothing to Ntoko about the incident as they travelled, although Mbile suspected that things had been said before they left and would be said again another day. Ntoko dozed most of the way, sitting close to Mbile in the back of the truck. He hadn't slept much the previous night, he said. As he dozed, he slumped against his father and, in spite of the rough road, it became a journey of contentment for Mbile.

There was no doubt that the whole incident had shaken up Ntoko quite badly. For a while he kept very much to himself, but he did visit Mbile a lot more than formerly. He seemed to appreciate being there in his old house and breathing in the atmosphere of the place again. He and Mbile talked together, although there was still a fair bit of reserve in the conversation. They never quite recaptured that moment of openness and heart-warming acceptance of each other that had occurred when Ntoko stepped out from between the two policeman to become a free man once again.

Gradually, more distance began to creep into their

relationship, despite all Mbile's efforts. For Mbile, it felt like a lovely fruit that had begun to wither in his hand. What Ntoko felt, he had no idea, but it was obvious that Ntoko was beginning to get his self-confidence back. He began to talk about the challenges facing the country, what needed to be done and what he would do if he had the power to do it, how there would be no need to live in poor houses any more, and so on. Mbile just listened, sometimes shaking his head a little as the words kept pouring out.

'You don't believe I could do all these things, do you?' said Ntoko. 'Well, I can and I will. You'll see.'

Mbile hadn't the heart to remind him of what had happened when he charged ahead to do something on his own a few weeks previously.

Then one day Ntoko said what Mbile had been preparing himself to hear. It had been building up to this, so when Ntoko came out with it, it was hardly a surprise, unwelcome though it was.

'I'm going back down to the big city. At the moment, this place is going nowhere and in any case, I need to continue my education.'

'Education?' said Mbile, taken aback because he hadn't thought of that as a reason for Ntoko going away. 'But you're already educated.'

Ntoko gave a snort by way of reply and explained to his father that going to university was something you had to do if you were going to get on in the world these days. As for the cost of doing this, Ntoko said he would manage, although he didn't say exactly how. Mbile said that he couldn't do much, but he could set up the arrangement with the local trader again, if that would be a help.

'Well, maybe to start with that would be good,' said Ntoko. 'I'll pay you back some day. You know that, don't you?'

And that was about all there was to it. Ntoko gave up his job and went downriver to the big city. Mbile went to the boat to see him off, wondering when Ntoko would be back home again, because he had implied several times that he wouldn't be back until he could do so as someone in authority. The river level had dropped since the day of his arrival, which meant that this time he had to get into a canoe and be paddled across to the boat. Mbile watched him scramble up onto the deck, then turn round and look back at the shore. Mbile waved and this time Ntoko waved back. That wave was something of a consolation to Mbile as he walked home.

Life settled back into its old routine. Mbile prayed for Ntoko every day, either as he sat outside his house in the early morning or when meeting with the others in the little chapel. It was the least he could do. He relived in his mind the events of the past few months when Ntoko had been around, wondering what more could have been done to build on the rare moment of real communication there had been between them. He tried to avoid harbouring any feelings of disappointment or hurt but sometimes as he sat and thought about things he would crack his knuckles, a sign of his inner tensions and frustration.

A visit to the local trader set up a renewed arrangement about money transfers to the big city, so that was something. Doing this made him feel that there was still a direct line of contact between him and Ntoko. Occasionally a letter would come from Ntoko. Mbile would reply, even although writing a letter was a slow and laborious business for him. He would tell Ntoko about the fishing or something about the neighbours or a little about his church activities or some improvements he was making to the house. He was sure it must seem like another world to Ntoko. Ntoko's letters never said very much about what he was doing, other than that he was well and that life was quite difficult – everything was so expensive. His letters were larded with French words, so much so that Mbile wondered why he bothered to write anything other than French. Sometimes Mbile even had to ask someone what a word meant and he felt foolish at being obliged to do so. He mentioned that in one letter, but it didn't seem to make any difference. Ntoko continued to write as before.

True to what he said, Ntoko did not come back home, even during holiday periods. After two years, Mbile did ask if he should come and visit him in the big city. He reckoned he might be able to rake together enough money for that. But Ntoko said he would be away from the city for several weeks at that time – something to do with his studies, he wrote – and it would be a wasted journey.

The year after that, however, Ntoko wrote to say that he was about to finish at university and had been given the opporunity to go to France to do his doctorate. Mbile had to ask someone what that meant because he was sure Ntoko wasn't training to be a doctor in a hospital. He was told that it was the sort of thing they gave to people who studied a bit more than others, and had nothing to do with hospitals.

'But all this education,' said Mbile, 'when's it going to stop? What's it all for?'

'It's what you do now if you're clever,' he was told. 'It's the way to the top. You'll see.'

What Ntoko suggested in the letter was that Mbile should come to the big city and that they should meet up before he went to France. He said that he might be in Europe for as long as four years. Mbile wrote back to say that yes, of course he would come and told him exactly when – in two weeks' time with the downriver boat.

'Will that be all right?' he wrote, and then as an afterthought he added, 'Do you want me to stop sending money to you now through the local trader? I don't think I could get money to you through him when you are in France.'

For once, Ntoko replied very promptly and said that Mbile shouldn't delay longer than two weeks, since he was waiting for news any day now about the date of his flight to France. 'But what's this about money coming to me through the local trader? I've never received anything.'

Mbile went to see the local trader to tell him he was going to the big city. After thinking about things, Mbile had decided that he didn't want to create any difficulties with the trader. To do so would only make his own life difficult, since the man would be bound to justify himself and turn the accusation against Mbile. Further, the local trader was very influential in the community and might cause Mbile all sorts of problems if he thought that he was been got at. So all that Mbile did was to ask the address of the local trader's brother in the big city and tell the local trader that he wouldn't be forwarding any more money to his son.

'Going to France, eh? Well, that's something,' said the local trader. 'He'll be a big man one day, that's for sure.'

'I don't know,' Mbile replied. 'He's going to be away for a very long time.'

'The longer he's away the higher he'll climb, believe me, I've seen it before.'

'I don't know,' said Mbile again, raising his eyebrows and peering out of the shop across the river into the distance as though France was somehow just out of view. 'I suppose I can still write to him.'

'Of course, you can. That's not a problem. Send him fish too.'

'Really?'

'Well maybe not, but probably other things,' said the local trader.

94

Coming away from the shop, Mbile felt sure the local trader hadn't deceived him. 'It must be his brother in the big city,' he said to himself, 'but I'll need to be very careful all the same. People in the big city can be very tricky and dangerous.'

There was no problem in getting leave from his work as a grass cutter. All that was left for him to do was to wait patiently for the day the boat would arrive. He packed one or two things in a bag, not forgetting his best shirt of course, and set aside a basket of his dried fish to go with him as a farewell gift for Ntoko. He could take it with him in the plane to France, he presumed.

On the day when the boat should have arrived, it did not come. This was hardly a surprise, especially with the down-river boat which was frequently late. Word eventually arrived that it had got stuck on a sandbank – a hazard at all times, but especially so in the dry season. There was nothing else to do but wait patiently. It would turn up at some point; it always did. This time it was three days late, which meant that the captain was cross, the passengers were cross and those waiting for the boat were cross. It made for a volatile mix. The captain wanted to be on his way. The passengers also wanted to be on their way, but at the same time have enough time to buy food and do business with the flotilla of canoes that had come out to meet the boat. Those waiting for the boat were panicking that the boat would not stop long enough for them to get themselves and all their multitude of goods on board – journeys to the big city were an opportunity for commerce, so people took fish and vegetables and any 'up-country delicacy' that they thought would sell well in the city.

Mbile managed to get on board without too much trouble, despite all the chaos around him, and found himself a space on the open deck of one of the passenger barges that the boat was pushing. He shared that space with a man who was one of his near neighbours and who made regular journeys to the big city as a trader.

After over twenty hours of travelling downstream, they saw the big city come into view and Mbile got ready for the meeting with Ntoko. He presumed Ntoko would be there to meet him. If there had been chaos when Mbile boarded the boat, this was multiplied several times over when the boat docked at the big city. Mbile wondered how he was going to be able to detect Ntoko in the mass of people that swarmed all over the boat and on the quayside. It was a confusion of people, boxes, baskets, crates of chickens, tethered bleating goats and even five live, bound crocodiles strapped to poles and eyeing the world in as much terror as people eyed them.

'I'll never find Ntoko in all this crowd,' he said to his neighbour.

'Don't worry. That's what everyone says,' replied his neighbour. 'It's amazing the way people do meet up and find each other. It happens all the time. Just stick with me and you'll be all right.'

But in this case the neighbour was wrong, because in spite of waiting for some time until the crowd began to thin out, they never did meet up with Ntoko.

'Something has happened to prevent him being here,' the neighbour said to Mbile. 'The best thing is for you to come with me and then we can go to where he is staying. You have the address?'

'Yes,' said Mbile. 'I have the address. It's the one I write to.

'Good then, there's no problem. We'll soon make contact.

For all his neighbour's optimism, Mbile sensed that there must be a problem and his heart sank a little at the thought He felt lost in the big city with its constant bustle of people trucks, cars and motorbikes, with roads going here and ther in bewildering profusion. He just had to rely on his neighbou to get him safely from one point to another. It was only later that day, however, that they managed to track down the place where Ntoko was living, which was quite near to the main university buildings. By the time they got there, Mbile's head was in a spin. The big city was too much for him and he wished that he was back home sitting under the shady tree in his yard whittling away at some of his forest creepers or even enjoying the steady rhythm of grass cutting in much quieter surroundings.

'Ah,' said a man they met at Ntoko's place, 'you must be Ntoko's father. He told me to keep a watch out for you. Just come off the river boat, have you?'

'Yes. It's three days late in getting here. Got caught on a sandbank.'

'Typical,' said the man. 'It's always happening. You would think a decent captain could avoid that. Anyway, you made it. But here, I've got a letter for you from Ntoko.' With that he pulled a letter from his pocket and handed it over to Mbile.

'Is Ntoko not here then?' asked Mbile, knowing in advance what the answer would be.

'No. He's up and off. Went a couple of days ago, I'm afraid. But I'm sure it's all there in the letter.'

Mbile held the letter in his hand and stared at it, until his neighbour-companion said that he would be better to read it and get things over with. So they walked away a little bit and shared the shade of a tired-looking tree with a young boy who was selling old car tyres, and a woman who was selling peanuts from a little rickety stall. The letter did indeed explain every-thing. The air ticket had come through and Ntoko had had to leave in a hurry. 'Very sorry not to have seen you,' he wrote. Mbile sighed and felt empty inside. At least this time it seemed that Ntoko wasn't to blame, but that didn't help very much to lessen Mbile's disappointment.

He bought some peanuts from the woman, who seemed delighted at the sale, and he said something encouraging to the boy selling the old tyres, before walking away with his neighbour. His neighbour said that there would be no problem if Mbile wished to stay where he was staying and Mbile accepted that invitation. He made up his mind to go back upriver as soon as possible, but not before he had gone to see the local trader's brother.

As it happened, the local trader's brother had his shop not too far from where Mbile was staying, so he was able to go there on his own. It was the kind of shop that looked as though it sold anything and everything, and it was busy with people. The local trader's brother was a big man with a loud booming voice and laugh. It was clear that business was very good indeed. Mbile wondered how he could bring up the subject of the monthly money transfers for Ntoko, but he needn't have worried because as soon as the local trader's brother knew who Mbile was, he shook him warmly by the hand and said what a pleasure it was to meet Ntoko's father after all these years.

'What is it? Six years that you've been sending money for Ntoko?'

'Nine,' said Mbile.

'Nine? Well there you are, I would never have believed it. I can remember when Ntoko came here as a young boy and it just seems like yesterday. And now he's off to France, lucky man.'

'Yes, he went three days ago. I've just missed seeing him.'

'Now isn't that bad luck. The last time I saw him was, let's see . . . probably three weeks ago when he came here for the money. Of course that will stop now. We've no relatives in France unfortunately!' he added with a guffaw.

'And he was last here three weeks ago?'

'Two or three, I can't quite remember. He's a fine man and

98

he's definitely going places, I can see that. And you've been an excellent father to him,' said the local trader's brother looking Mbile up and down and noting his rough hands and rather shabby, 'up-country' appearance. It spoke of little surplus money being around.

Mbile was confused. How could he say to this man that he hadn't handed any money over to Ntoko for the last three years. Or was it that Ntoko . . .? In the end, all he could do was to look the man straight in the face and thank him for being such a help over the years. There was no hint of embarrassment in the shopkeeper's eyes, but then big city shopkeepers and businessmen could be such rogues. Mbile was glad to get away from the shop. This was something that he would just have to let be. He was not going to pursue the matter any further – either here with the local trader's brother or with Ntoko when he wrote to him.

Two days later, Mbile left on the upriver boat, leaving the basket of dried fish that he had brought for Ntoko with his neighbour.

'You can eat it or sell it,' he said to his neighbour. 'Without you I would have been in a real mess in this city. I can't see me coming back here in a hurry.'

'Not until Ntoko is a government minister, that is,' laughed his neighbour.

'Not even then,' said Mbile.

Back home from the big city, Mbile immersed himself in his work and his fishing without trying to ask himself too many times why things had turned out as they had. His deep-rooted belief in God was a help, and to listen to him praying in the little chapel you would never have guessed the hidden hurts within him. People merely noted how composed and calm he was about everything and how he always replied with such careful politeness that Ntoko was very well indeed, whenever someone asked him how his son was getting on.

Letters from Ntoko became a rarity and Mbile's own letters to Ntoko were infrequent. It cost money to send letters to Europe for one thing, and then after a few letters describing what he was doing, what else was there to write about? Then came the news in one of Ntoko's letters that he was going to get married This was a couple of years into Ntoko's doctoral studies. It appeared that the girl he was going to marry had been married before to another doctoral student, but this man had left her for some other woman. There had been a divorce. However, the deserted wife was doing some studies of her own and she wanted to be able to stay on in France.

So Ntoko married her. It was most irregular. No consultation with families. No testing out whether or not everything was in order. No waiting for approval. Instead, it had all been done by Ntoko and the woman and their fellow students. This was not how it should be, Mbile said to himself. How will they be able to stay together properly if their families have been excluded from the marriage arrangements? And then, to add to the complications, the woman came from a different part of the country. Her customs and traditions would be different from Ntoko's. It was a real problem. If only Ntoko would use all his education to act responsibly But the wedding had taken place and there was no going back on it. At least the woman had had no children by her first husband in their brief married life together, so that was something of a consolation.

News about Ntoko's wedding got out. That was inevitable and Mbile had to find ways of replying to people when they asked him about it.

'Is it right what I hear that Ntoko's got married?'

'Yes. About a month ago in France.'

'From a family we know?'

'No. She's from down near the big city originally. She's a student too.'

'Well what a surprise.'

'Yes. It's because they are in France for such a long time. They weren't able to do things in the traditional way. These sort of things happen in Europe, you know.'

'But not to know about it. How do you feel about that?'

At that point Mbile would try to reassure people that he accepted it and looked forward to meeting his daughter-in-law, although within himself he felt that it was all very wrong. Eventually a photo of Ntoko and his new wife, Philomene, arrived. Mbile had to admit that she did look a nice and attractive girl, even though she was made up in a European way. Maybe it would turn out all right in the end.

By the time Ntoko finished his studies and got his doctorate – he did very well apparently – another two years had passed and a little baby girl had been born. The family was expecting to return home to the big city, when Ntoko was contacted by the government to go to Paris and do something in the embassy there. Mbile had no idea what it was, and had to be vague when answering people's questions. Letters from Ntoko got even rarer. Mbile felt like someone on a long hard journey, walking and walking in the hope that he would get to a place where he could stop and rest. Never a day passed without him thinking about Ntoko and his family, and living with a dull ache in his heart.

A year and a half after the move to Paris, Ntoko and Philomene, along with their two children – a boy had been added to their family – did indeed return to the big city. All Ntoko said in his letter was that he had been given a job to do by the President, but he didn't say what it was. He said that he hoped to see Mbile again soon. Mbile took a big breath when he read that, and for the first time in all these eight-and-a-half years of waiting, his eyes filled with tears.

It was two or three days later, when he was at the local trader's shop, that he got more news about Ntoko. He had just entered the shop when the local trader spied him and in a voice just about as loud as his brother's in the big city, said, 'I told you it would happen. Congratulations.'

Mbile looked startled.

'It was on the radio this morning, didn't you hear it?' the local trader went on in an excited cheerful voice which had everybody in the shop turning to look at Mbile.

'Hear what?' said Mbile, feeling a bit confused.

'Hear about Ntoko, of course. He's a new government minister. The President announced it yesterday afternoon. Minister Ntoko – I always knew it.'

People gathered round and shook Mbile's hand and you could see it written in their eyes that Mbile was now someone to be respected and not to be crossed. 'His son's a government minister,' they would say. 'You ought to keep on the right side of Mbile from now on.'

Mbile got away from the shop as quickly he could and made his way home. News seemed to have spread fast. People smiled and waved to him and shouted out greetings as he walked along the road. He knew he should be feeling absolutely delighted, but he couldn't quite get the feeling going. Instead, he felt nervous and apprehensive for Ntoko.

Rumours began to circulate that now that Ntoko was a government minister he was going to do all sorts of things to help the area he came from. People got quite excited about it. Mbile even had a visit from the local State Administrator one evening – out for a gentle evening stroll, he said, and by chance there was Mbile's house right before him.

'Everything going all right with you?'

'Yes, I'm just fine,' said Mbile.

'Well, if you do have any problems, you know that you can come and see me at any time, don't you? I'd only be too glad to help.'

'Thank you,' Mbile replied, trying not to show his embarrassment. He could see that a good number of his neighbours were watching what was happening with considerable interest. 'I don't have any problems at the moment.'

'Well, if you do, let me know,' said the State Administrator as he turned away to continue his evening stroll. Then he stopped, as if on the spur of the moment, to add, 'And how's your son by the way? I suppose you'll be seeing him soon. We're all delighted that he is now a government minister and we're expecting great things from him, of course.'

That and similar remarks by others only made Mbile feel even more nervous. These feelings were heightened when he had a letter from Ntoko telling him not to come down to the big city – something that Mbile was preparing to do, despite his dislike of the place. Ntoko said that he would be making a visit home just as soon as he could find a couple of free days. Mbile didn't know whether to feel joy or not. Yes, he wanted to see Ntoko. Of course he did. But all these things people were saying to him about what Ntoko might be able to do for them now, made him wish that he and Ntoko could meet away from all that kind of fuss. He wished too that he could banish the recurring image of Ntoko standing barefoot between two policemen all these years ago, when he had tried to make a big impression on that place inland. But try as he might, it kept coming back. When it did, all Mbile could do was shut his eyes, say, 'Please God, no,' and leave it at that.

For everybody around Mbile, Ntoko's visit was a huge success. He had arrived in none other than the President's helicopter.

'See. I told you this would happen,' quite a few folks said, pleased that they had got it right after all. 'He's a really big man now.'

Mbile had been invited by the local State Administrator to be there when the helicopter landed. This time he had on his best shirt, as befitted his position as a government minister's father. When the helicopter blades had stopped turning, the door slid open and Ntoko stepped out to the applause of everyone there – and there was a big crowd. Ntoko, looking very smart in his light tropical suit – 'that cost a bit,' said a few discerning experts – took a few steps away from the helicopter and then raised his hands to applaud the applause he was receiving. He had put on a bit of weight, Mbile noticed, and was sporting a dapper-looking moustache, but it was still the same Ntoko.

Mbile waited. This time he was not going to run the risk of any rejection by pushing himself forward and maybe embarrassing Ntoko again. So he didn't move from where he was standing. But there was nothing to stop him smiling and his whole face lit up with delight.

Ntoko saw him immediately and smiled back. People saw that and liked what they saw. They liked it even more when, after shaking hands with the local State Administrator and those with him, Ntoko turned and made straight for Mbile.

'Papa,' he said 'it's me. I've come back.'

To which all that a misty eyed Mbile could say was 'My child.'

There was more applause at that and even cheering by the crowd. This was the stuff of dreams – your son coming back in a helicopter as a government minister. Ntoko acknowledged the applause yet again and then raised his hand for silence. He told them how glad he was to be back with them and that he had come to see what could be done to improve their living condi tions – further great applause and more acknowledgement by Ntoko. Mbile hardly heard anything he said, but his eyes never left Ntoko's face. How he wished Nselibeka had been there.

The two days of Ntoko's stay went by in a flash. He didn't stay with Mbile, but was the guest of the local State Administrator. Most of his time was spent speaking to people who wanted to see him and get him to help them, but he did manage to come to his old home in the evening and talk with Mbile. It wasn't entirely satisfactory because he came with a group of his people and a couple of policemen to protect him – from what? thought Mbile. Ntoko seemed to be concerned about the state of the house.

'We'll have to do something about this,' he said, 'can't have my father living like this.'

'Oh, I'm all right,' said Mbile. 'It suits me fine. I'm used to it.'

'No, it's got to be improved,' said Ntoko. 'Leave it to me.' He gave some kind of order to one of the men accompanying him. There were a few approving nods all round. Just as it should be. It would reflect badly on a government minister if his father wasn't taken care of.

Ntoko would have liked to sit down and talk with Ntoko at leisure. There was a lot he wanted to know. All about Philomene and the two children – his grandchildren after all – and what it had been like in France. What he had learned and seen when he was there and . . . and . . . well there were so many things. Above all he would have liked just to sit with Ntoko and come at everything in a relaxed way, letting the conversation go this way and that as the mood took them, as though out on the river fishing while the canoe drifted gently on the current. But that didn't happen. Ntoko was back in the President's helicopter on the afternoon of his second day there and the visit was over.

'You must come and see me and the family soon,' said Ntoko. 'I'll let you know when it will be convenient.'

Then he was off. The Government Minister speeding back to big things in the big city.

Before leaving, Ntoko sent a man to Mbile who gave him a brown envelope with money in it. Inside the envelope there was a note from Ntoko which merely said *For putting in the tin box*. Mbile smiled when he read that. At least it showed that Ntoko had a sense of humour and had not forgotten the past completely. He was grateful for the money, but would gladly have had less money and a bit more time with Ntoko if he had had the choice.

It wasn't long before the first consignment of things arrived by boat – construction material, in the main, for the new jetty that Ntoko had promised to see built, along with pipes for a clean water project, metal bars and girders for something to do with that project and, of course, many bags of cement.

It was very impressive. There were even roofing sheets in abundance, some of which were carried to Mbile's house and work carried out on the house as Ntoko had ordered. People spoke about it all with real pride in the story of 'the local boy made good' and looked forward to further consignments arriving – which they did.

Mbile remained just as he always had been – quiet, digni-fied, cutting the grass, going fishing, praying in the mornings at the little chapel, putting on his best shirt for the big communion services in the main church, and shaking his head gently when people praised him for having such a wonderful son. Within him, he wondered what would happen in the end, and he waited for word from Ntoko to go downriver to the big city to see him.

The wait to go to the big city lasted for some time. Ntoko seemed to be very busy going here and there on government business. Letters from him seemed to dry up and were replaced by unsatisfactory brief messages that came to Mbile through the local State Administrator as additions to official communications. They were usually 'All well. Will be in touch soon. Hope you're well' sort of messages. In the meantime, the new jetty was built and some digging began for the clean water project. Mbile couldn't quite work out what had happened to some of the material, all the same. He feared that things were going missing. Did Ntoko and the government know that was happening, he wondered? Presumably it was Government money that had bought all these things.

Mbile became even more anxious one day when he overheard two men talking at the market.

'Our friend Ntoko must be making a fortune out of all this,' said one man.

'You can say that again,' said the other, 'but he had better be careful. Someone will find out sooner or later and then there'll be trouble. You'll see.'

Mbile moved away quickly before the men could see him. He went back to work with more to worry about. The picture of Ntoko standing barefoot between two policemen kept on coming back to him during the rest of that day. It unsettled him.

'Are you all right?' his employer asked him.

'Yes, I'm fine. A bit of a headache. A little fever probably.'

'Well, take the rest of the day off and go to the hospital for some medicine.'

'No, it'll go away. I'd rather just keep on working.'

The rhythmic cutting of the grass helped to steady his feelings, Mbile found. That night, however, he prayed even more earnestly for Ntoko.

There were several weeks after that when he got no news at all of Ntoko. Then the friend who had helped him on his first and only visit to the big city turned up one night to see him and give him a letter. He seemed ill at ease, only waiting long enough to say that a man had given him this letter in the big city to take to Mbile, with instructions that he shouldn't say anything about it to anyone. Mbile recognised Ntoko's handwriting on the envelope.

Having read the letter, Mbile sat with his head down, trying to take it all in. Ntoko was unwell. Seriously unwell. He had been out of the country for four weeks – that would explain the absence of news – but now he was back in the big city. He had had an operation on his throat in another country and the President had paid for it. He really ought to go back to that country for a follow-up operation, but things had happened when he was away and he was now no longer a government minister. The President was not interested in him any longer. There were other things that he couldn't write about, he said, but could Mbile come and see him?

'I need to see you, Papa,' he wrote. 'I need to talk to you.'

Mbile went down to the big city on that week's boat. By then it was known that Ntoko was no longer a government minister and people were puzzled. The place was full of rumours. Some of them were nasty ones as well. Work stopped on the clean water project and people who had been ingratiating themselves with Mbile avoided him.

'What's happened to Ntoko?' people asked him.

'He's very ill,' was all that Mbile could say. 'I'm going to see him.'

The big city was no more attractive to Mbile on this visit than it was previously. The downriver boat was just as crowded as before and the chaos at the big city's quayside seemed even worse. Although he knew quite a few people who were travelling downriver on the boat, Mbile preferred to keep himself to himself this time. Once in the big city, he got a taxi. Thanks to Ntoko's brown envelope, there was plenty of money in the little tin box for this expense. The taxi took him straight to Ntoko's house in one of the better-off parts of the city.

Mbile didn't know what to expect. He had never met Philomene nor seen his grandchildren. There were a number of people hanging about outside the house, some of whom Mbile recognised as coming from his area, and who recognised him in return. One of them went into the house and told Ntoko that his father had arrived, but it was Philomene rather than Ntoko who came out to welcome him. She was a good-looking woman, Mbile could see that, dressed quite fashionably – all those years in France told – and she smiled at Mbile. There was both welcome and sadness in the smile and her eyes filled with tears. 'Come in,' she said, reaching out to touch Mbile. 'Ntoko's waiting for you, Papa.'

Mbile didn't know what to say to her. She had called him 'Papa'. She was the mother of his grandchildren, but he had never met her before. His only reply was to look at her and say gently, 'I came as soon as I could.'

Ntoko was sitting in a big armchair on an upstairs veranda – the house seemed huge. He got up slowly when he saw Mbile, his eyes fixed on those of his father. So much was conveyed in that look. It seemed to hold within it the story of the years, coloured now by despair and appeal. Mbile was shocked at his appearance, but tried not to show it. Clutching his throat, Ntoko croaked out some words of greeting but Mbile said nothing. Instead, he stepped forward and embraced Ntoko. They held onto each other in silence, each too moved to say anything.

Once seated and with their emotions under control, they talked. It was a strange story that Ntoko had to tell. Talking wasn't easy. Every time he wanted to say anything, he had to grip his throat. He had an opening in his neck which, he explained to Mbile, was the result of a tracheotomy done in the hospital in the other country. He had had to learn to speak in a different way and could only do so if he closed the opening in his neck as he spoke. This meant that he couldn't say much at any one time and he got tired easily. Mbile told him to take his time – he was not in any hurry.

Ntoko's claim was that he had been deliberately poisoned by something he had eaten or drunk at a presidential reception. Before the end of the reception he had felt a burning sensation in his throat and this had worsened when he got home. The next day, and in the days after that, there was no change in his condition. Word came to him from the President that he was to fly immediately to another country to get some treatment and this is what he had done. No one mentioned the word 'poisoning', but that was the implication all along – he could see it in the doctors' faces. But then, who had done the poisoning? No one dared say. He came back to the big city because the President had recalled him and, despite the protests of the doctors where he was being treated, Ntoko insisted on leaving. So he left, even although his tracheotomy remained unreversed.

'I'll return,' he said, 'the President will want that I'm sure.'

But the President hadn't wanted that, as it turned out. During Ntoko's absence, claims were made by some people that Ntoko had been siphoning off government money from the elaborate development projects he had authorised for his home area and that, in that area, he was a bigger personality for the local population than the President himself. The President listened to all of this and decided that Ntoko should be discarded. He was recalled immediately to the big city, with all financial help for his treatment withdrawn. When told how ill Ntoko was, the President merely shrugged his shoulders and said, 'Too bad.'

Telling this story took some time. It was agonising for Mbile to listen to it, yet he sat there with his heart full of gratitude to God that he and Ntoko were together and talking to each other at last with no barriers between them. He said that to Ntoko, but Ntoko shook his head.

'God?' he said, 'God? Where's God in all this? Why has this happened to me when I still have so much to offer in life?'

Mbile felt there must be an answer to that question, because God had always meant so much to him, but he had no words to explain what his heart felt was true about God. Instead, by way of reply, all he could do was to reach out and grip Ntoko's hand and say, 'Calm your heart, child of mine. Calm your heart.'

There is not a great deal to add. Mbile stayed with Ntoko and Philomene for two months as Ntoko got weaker. He got to know his two grandchildren and made clever things with his hands that delighted them. He and Ntoko continued to talk when Ntoko was up to it – all about the past and Ntoko's childhood and stories about Nselibeka and about fishing and the river and even grass cutting. Each morning Mbile prayed with Ntoko – a big-city, big-house version of the little chapel prayers beside Mbile's house.

After Ntoko died, Mbile stayed on a little longer with Philomene and the children before they went to live with her parents. Three months after leaving on his second visit to the big city, he was back home. People called to say how sorry they were about Ntoko's death and there were many who assured him that Ntoko had been honest in setting up the development projects. It was just that he had political enemies down in the big city. A dreadful place.

Then one day he had a visit from the local trader. That was a surprise. The local trader told him that his brother in the big city had been unwell. He had been in hospital for some weeks. Apparently he had had plenty of time to think about things and he wanted to set something straight with Mbile. Having told Mbile all this, the local trader handed over a bulky package – the three years of money transfers that the brother had failed to hand over to Ntoko.

'He is deeply sorry about this,' said the local trader, 'and especially so after hearing about Ntoko's tragic death.'

Mbile took the package and with a little shake of his head said, 'Send him my thanks. He's done well and so have you in coming to see me. It helps me to know that Ntoko wasn't at fault in this.'

They shook hands. The local trader returned to his shop, leaving Mbile the grass-cutter, fisherman and bereaved father, watching him go. He stood there for a moment or two, quiet and dignified as always and seemingly deep in thought, before taking the package into his house and putting it in the tin box.

The Unusual Conspiracy

Always, Sir, set a high value on spontaneous kindness.
Dr. Samuel Johnson in Boswell's *Life*

We pass on what we learn, and from both of you I learned that kindness is the greatest virtue.
Fergal Keane about his parents in *All of these People*

The trouble with dying when you are a hundred and two years old is that there are few, if any, of your peers left to corroborate or deny the nice things that people feel obliged to say about you after you are gone. That's how it seemed to me at old Uncle John's funeral. I was twenty-two at the time and had gone there as one of the few remaining representatives of the family. Given that old Uncle John was actually my grandmother's uncle, you would have expected him to have had quite a tail of descendants trailing after him, but he and his wife had had no children and his brother, my grandmother's father, had only done marginally better than him – one child to him and my great-grandmother, two to my grandparents and then just me after that. We are a family in danger of dying out, it would appear.

So at the funeral there were just four others of the family apart from twenty-two-year-old me – my grandmother (sadly, at the age of only seventy-four, a widow of several years by then), my parents and my father's unmarried sister, Aunt Jane – all in their late forties. I hope you are still with me. Family genealogies can be so complicated and boring to others, I find, but I thought I had better explain all this at the very start so that you can get some sort of generational time-frame for our family.

The funeral service was held in the residential home where old Uncle John had been for quite a number of years. It wasn't a very nice day, but the sitting room where we gathered looked restful, with flowers and taped background music to create a suitably solemn atmosphere. I suppose the people in charge must have been used to all this, with somebody ticking a list of things to do when a resident died – a wearisome, organisational repetition for them, no doubt, but impressive enough for the bereaved families.

You could hardly say that we, as the bereaved family, were plunged into the deepest of grief. I had only visited the old man a couple of times in my life – once when I was still at primary school and once on his hundredth birthday. In fact, when I come to think about it, the first occasion must have been on his ninetieth birthday. As a ten-year-old on the first of these visits, all I remember registering was that this was a very old man.

'Uncle, this is John,' said my grandmother to the old man as she steered me in his direction, 'the same name as you.'

With this I found myself manoeuvred by my grandmother into a seat beside this ancient relative of mine. I can't remember anything he said to me on that occasion. What I do remember was his hand resting on my arm as he spoke. There were blotches on the skin and the veins stood out, I recall, while the fingers seemed taper-thin to me. He then drew my boy's hand into his and held it there for a bit, letting his thumb play over the back of my hand. I remember finding it strangely soothing and affirming in a way I couldn't describe. His touch seemed to be telling me that he was on my side and wished me well. Maybe that's why I can't remember anything he said. I didn't need his words. He had said it all as he held my hand. Possibly I am reading back into that encounter things about old Uncle John that I picked up later on. That said, however, the memory of his hand enclosing my hand has stayed with me, so it must have made a deep impression.

As for his hundredth birthday 'do' ten years later, I almost forgot to be there.

'It would be nice if you could come,' my mother had said to me over the phone, and I had replied that I would try to make it, even though it was going to mean quite a long journey. A couple of days before the event another phone call from my mother reminded me that I had forgotten about the whole thing. It meant cancelling something I had already fixed up for that day, and it was with little good grace that I went back home to my parents' house to spend a night there, before getting a lift with them the following day to where old Uncle John was living.

As it turned out, on the day of his big birthday old Uncle John was not very well and he had to spend the day confined to bed. This hardly made for an uproarious birthday party, but we did gather in his room and sing Happy Birthday, standing beside a nice cake that my mother had baked and brought with her. On this occasion I do remember what old Uncle John said to me, as I shook his even more aged-looking, crinkly hand. He looked up at me from the bed and with a quaint little nod of his head said, 'How kind of you to come. Thank you so much.'

I muttered something about how pleased I was to be there and tried to forget all the complaints I had made to my parents about the inconvenience of it all.

Possibly it was some lingering guilt about my reluctance to be at the hundredth birthday celebrations that made me respond very quickly to the news about old Uncle John's death two years later.

'Yes, of course, I'll be there,' I said on the phone, when my father hinted strongly that it would be good if I could make it.

'There are really very few of us in the family, as you know so . . .'

'No, it's not a problem, I'll be there,' I said again.

So it was, then, that I sat in the residents' sitting room of the care home on that fairly bleak day and listened to a local minister conduct a brief funeral service. He said some nice things about old Uncle John, even though on his own admission he had only got to know him during the last two or three years. Not enough time to really know him, I thought to myself, but then who was I to talk? At the post-funeral get-together, which we had in a nearby local hotel, there was some reminiscing about old Uncle John by my grandmother, but on her own admission she knew surprisingly little about his life. She did know, however, that he had once lived and worked in Brazil when he was a young man.

'Came back home in the middle of the First World War and was drafted into the army more or less straight away. There was some story or other about why he left Brazil, but my father never spoke about it, or if he did, I must have paid little attention to it. In any case I was only about seven at the time and when Uncle John came out of the army at the end of the war he went to live down in Dorset where he eventually met and married my aunt. We never really saw him after that, except on the occasional visit that he made north. I think he had been gassed or something in the war and felt that he ought to live in part of the country where there was a milder climate. It was something of a surprise when he came back north and moved into the care home after my aunt died.'

As we sat and talked in the hotel restaurant, my grandmother recounted one or two more inconsequential stories revolving around his visits north to her family, but there was nothing out of the ordinary. He appeared to have been a consistently kind sort of man, with a strong religious faith that had stayed with him to the end of his days. The minister who conducted the funeral service had spoken about that quite eloquently and to me it had sounded genuine enough.

So that was old Uncle John, born 1881 died 1983, formerly of Brazil, ex-First World War soldier, resident of Dorset for most of his life. A nice man. A kind man. Another life lived and now over. Time to move on, as memory of him slipped quietly into the gentle haze of forgetfulness. And that's how it would have been, no doubt, if that dusty cardboard box hadn't come my way twenty-five years later as I was beginning to see my fiftieth birthday looming up in a couple of years. I suppose at this age you begin to get more interested in your roots, which is why I found myself fascinated by what I discovered in the box.

It had belonged to old Uncle John and it came to me on the death of my Aunt Jane, my father's sister. She was always one for hoarding and storing things, which is probably why my grandmother, who must have got the box from the care home when her uncle died, had given it to Aunt Jane rather than to my father − my mother was a renowned thrower-out of things, so the box might not have lasted too long if it had come into my parents' house. My grandmother died back in 1994, so the box had been gathering dust in one of Aunt Jane's cupboards for fourteen years. I'm not sure why I am giving you all this detail, but that's the way I am − I like to get everything laid out straight and in line, so that I can see where all the tie-ups are.

Aunt Jane's death in her early seventies was a very sad time for my parents and me − now the only surviving members of our family. I have never married, in case you are wondering. But I mustn't dwell on this, other than to reflect that once again life showed itself to be a passing experience for us all, raising questions about what we do with it. Maybe this was what stimulated my interest in the cardboard box because traditionally, dusty old cardboard boxes hidden away in cupboards for years on end invariably hold some secrets.

must have said something like this to my father, who told me that I should take the box if I wanted it. Not being a great family historian, he said that at the age of seventy-four he was not proposing to become one. 'So, over to you!' he said. The box, then, came to stay with me.

There were a variety of things in the box – the odds and ends that anyone collects over a lifetime and which, for sentimental reasons, must be preserved. The hundredth birthday cards were there, as was the Order of Service for his wedding back in 1920 – he would have been thirty-nine years old then, I calculated quickly. A little box contained his wife's wedding ring, with the engraving still legible on the inside. I held the ring in my hand for a bit and wondered how he had felt all those years ago, as he slipped it on to his new wife's finger. He was no youngster coming to marriage in the flush of his early twenties. Had he thought of this day many times before in previous years and wondered if it would ever happen? Another little white box held his First World War service medals. I looked at them and, to my surprise, saw that one of them was the Military Medal given for valour. No one had told me about that. I presumed this must have been something he got in the gassing incident that my grandmother mentioned. So this was a brave man, I thought, as I looked at a photo of him and a friend in their army uniforms, finding it difficult to see the man in the photo as related to the ninety-year-old who had held my boy's hand in his thirty-five years ago. His Bible and an old hymn book were there, the Bible obviously well used and heavily underlined in places. There was a little cloth bag with some small stones – gathered from some beach somewhere. There was a map of the London Underground and a ticket for a concert which he must have attended at the old Queen's Hall in November 1929. It was a treasure trove of personal memorabilia – the sort of thing he probably looked

at every so often as he cleared things out and which was always
given a reprieve for at least another few years

It was at the bottom of the box that I came across a bulky,
faded, brown-paper package tied up in string. I knew in my
bones, when I saw it, that this was going to be interesting,
but I never imagined where it would end up taking me in a
few months' time. I undid the string and carefully opened
the package. It was a pile of handwritten letters. The writing
wasn't very easy to decipher, but straight away I saw that
they were not in English. I'm not a linguist, but I was pretty
certain that what I was trying to read was Portuguese – it
would fit, in any case, given old Uncle John's years in Brazil.
The letters had all been taken out of their envelopes and tied
together, but at the bottom of the pile there was an off-white,
stained envelope which I picked up but didn't open instantly.
I held it in my hands for a moment or two and smiled at
what I thought I was going to find inside. I suspected that it
held a photograph. I opened it very carefully and there was
indeed a photograph, plus a lock of dark hair wrapped up
in a piece of tissue paper. The sepia-coloured photo was of
a slim, olive-skinned young woman with luxurious black hair
falling over the shoulders of her white dress. She was smiling
at the camera.

So this must have been old Uncle John's Brazilian girlfriend,
fiancée, wife even. No doubt the letters were from her and
would reveal everything. I closed the cardboard box – I would
have to decide what to do with the other things later – but I
kept out the letters and the envelope with the photo and lock
of hair in it. What I needed now was to get someone to translate the letters for me and, fortunately, this was not difficult to
arrange. I had a friend married to a Brazilian and Suzana was
only too happy to help out when I asked her.

'Give me a day or two,' she said, 'and I will at least give

you the gist of what the letters say. Mind you, the writing isn't too clear, but I'll do my best.'

I showed her the photo, of course, and she said what a beautiful young woman it was. With a laugh, she asked me if I wanted all the passionate bits of the letters translated, 'you being such a romantic, passionate man yourself'. I said, 'the gist . . . the gist . . . that will do,' and she laughed again and gave me a friendly hug.

It was about a week later that Suzana came on the phone to apologise for the delay in contacting me, but to tell me that she had been through the letters and had found them to be quite a surprise.

'What kind of surprise?' I asked.

Suzana gave a sort of evasive answer and said that it was too complicated to explain everything over the phone, so would I be free next Tuesday evening to join Jim and her for a meal? I was free, as it happened, and that's why the following Tuesday evening after a delicious Brazilian meal – a change from my more humble bachelor fare – Jim, Suzana and I sat together in their lounge with old Uncle John's letters lying on the coffee table in front of us.

'All right then,' I said, 'tell me all about them and get me out of my suspense.'

Suzana had insisted that we should wait till after the meal was over before discussing the letters, but now she was ready to tell me what she had found out.

'Well,' she said, looking at me with a tight little smile, 'the first thing to tell you is that these letters were not from a woman, and the second thing to tell you is that most of them were written by an inmate in a Sao Paulo State prison.'

'And the . . .' I began to say.

'. . . and the photo,' said Suzana, completing the sentence for me, 'that is what is at the centre of it all.'

121

The evening turned out to be a cross between a lesson from Suzana on the history of Brazil in the early part of the twentieth century and a sketchy putting together of events in old Uncle John's life from information in the letters lying in front of us.

The writer of the letters was a man called Pedro and as far as we could make out, he seemed to have gone to prison somewhere around 1912 or 1913. What appeared to be the first letter was a peculiar kind of 'acknowledgement letter' for the gift of some food and a pair of shoes that he had received from old Uncle John. It was a brief letter in which, Suzana said, Pedro told old Uncle John not to send any more things to him but to forget him entirely – 'Just leave me alone. I don't want anything to do with you,' he had written.

The second letter was even more angry in tone than the first, as old Uncle John had apparently not heeded what had been said in the first and had sent some more things to Pedro.

I could see that we were in for a very long evening if we were going to go through all the letters one by one and I said that to Jim and Suzana. They agreed. So I asked Suzana if she had been able to piece together anything of the story behind these letters and where the young woman in the photo came in. She said that quite a lot came out in some of the later letters, when Pedro had mellowed in his replies and begun to accept, albeit reluctantly at first, the repeated acts of kindness of old Uncle John. Having said that, she picked up the pile of letters and ruffled through them until she came to one that she had obviously marked out specially to show me. Although the writing had faded, Suzana thought it had been written in about 1914, which meant that by then Pedro must have been in prison for around two years. Her finger pointing to some lines halfway down the page, Suzana read out, first in Portuguese and then in English, these words:

'You have been a good friend to me. I don't deserve that. For your sake and my sake, how I wish I hadn't pulled the trigger that day and killed her. I curse the day I was caught up in the José Maria uprising.'

None of us spoke for a moment. I took the stained white envelope with the young woman's photo in it, drew out the photo and laid it on the table. I did the same with the tissue paper containing the lock of hair, feeling the hair between my finger and thumb as I did so. There was a sharp poignancy to the moment as we saw them lying alongside the letter of the man who was now regretting that he had cut short their owner's life all those years ago.

'So he shot her,' I said. Suzana and Jim just nodded, their eyes, like mine, fixed on the photo and the lock of hair.

It was at this point that the history lesson began, because obviously I wanted to know who this José Maria person was, how it came about that the girl in the photo had been shot in the uprising, what old Uncle John was doing at the time and what the girl had meant to him.

'Hang on,' said Suzana, who spoke pretty good idiomatic English. 'I can't answer all these questions at once and, in any case, these letters still don't tell us all the details of what happened.'

She did know quite a bit about the José Maria rebellion, however, and I found that very interesting. Apparently José Maria, whose real name was Miguel Lucena Boaventura, was a kind of wandering monk who captured people's allegiance by his healings and simple way of life. In fact he was the third 'José Maria' to appear as a wandering monk within the space of forty years or so and some people believed that he was the original José Maria come back to life again. He certainly had a big following from 1912 onwards in the southern part of Brazil in the states of Parana and Santa Caterina. All this was at a time when the expansion of the railways was taking place in Brazil and there had been a major project to build a railway from Sao Paulo down into the most southern state of Rio Grande do Sul. It was estimated that something like 8000 men came from different parts of Brazil to work on the railway, some of them from as far north as Recife.

'And Pedro was one of those?' I asked.

'Yes, I think so,' said Suzana. 'He seemed to have come from Recife because in one of his later letters he refers to his family being there.'

'And the girl?'

'That's not so easy to answer,' Suzana went on, 'but I think she came from Parana or maybe from Sao Paulo. She was certainly buried in Parana because Pedro asks your Uncle to put flowers on her grave at Rio Negro – a place right on the border with Santa Caterina.'

Suzana leafed through the letters again and came up with one dated 30th March 1915 in which he made that special request to old Uncle John – 'When you visit the grave on Easter Day in five days' time.'

'Anyway, what happened?' I said, 'I mean about the shooting.'

'Well, I think it must have happened at the time of a battle between government soldiers and José Maria's followers around October or November 1912,' Suzana replied.

She went on to tell me that there had been general unhappiness about the way the railway company had dispossessed people of their land for many kilometres on either side of the railway. These disgruntled people had been joined by Pedro and many of his work colleagues when the railway company didn't honour some of its agreements. José Maria had turned up at that point and served as a rallying figure to give focus to the unrest. The clash with soldiers at the beginning of the Contestado War, as it was called – a war that went on for another four years – saw many people killed, including José Maria himself.

'Somehow this young woman was killed on that day,' Suzana said.

'But how? And where was old Uncle John at this time?' I asked.

Unfortunately, the letters didn't do much to answer either of these questions, apart from making it clear that the death of the young woman in the photo had been something of an accident and that my old Uncle John had been there at the time. In one of the letters near the bottom of the pile, Pedro had referred back to the shooting and written about how much sorrow it must have brought to old Uncle John – 'The shot was meant for you, as you know. You must have wished that it had hit you and not the girl. When I saw what had happened, I just ran away and continued my flight to safety. As you know, I was caught by pursuing soldiers only two hours later and barely escaped with my own life.'

It appeared that Pedro had been at the 'battle' and once the fight had swung in favour of the soldiers he had fled, taking a pot shot on the way at someone whom he suspected was one of the railroad operators, standing with a young woman at his side.

'If Pedro knew old Uncle John would understand that the shot was intended for him, then I presume old Uncle John really was one of the railroad operators,' I said.

Suzana agreed that that was very likely. Quite a number of North Americans and Europeans had been enlisted by the railroad company – young men like my old Uncle John, prepared to live rough and keep on the move. But who the young woman was remained a mystery, except that Pedro in his letters was assuming she was someone special to old Uncle John. You don't go visiting a grave at Rio Negro three years after a death without the person buried there being 'someone special'.

Suzana, Jim and I continued to talk and speculate together about what had happened all these years ago, until I looked at my watch and said that I really must go home. I thanked them for all their help and promised to keep them informed of anything more that I could find out about old Uncle John.

'Are you quite sure there is nothing else in the old cardboard box?' Suzana said as a parting shot. I said that I would have another careful look, but I was not too hopeful of finding anything significant that I had overlooked.

Well, you know how it is, once you are on the track of something you don't like the scent to grow cold, so as soon as I was back home I got out the cardboard box again and rummaged through its contents. Just to make sure, I tipped them all out onto the table so that I wouldn't miss anything.

Everything was just as before – the medals, the concert programme, the wedding Order of Service, the wedding ring, the cloth bundle of stones, the hundredth birthday cards and the other odds and ends that I had already checked out. I was a bit disappointing, but then it was a long shot anyway, told myself. I put everything back into the box, with the birthday cards the last to go in. Then it occurred to me that I hadn't really looked properly at these cards. The one from my parents was on the top, then one or two from people I didn't know – presumably old friends from Dorset – and then there was rather ornate card below that. My heart skipped a beat when I saw it, because it was a Portuguese greeting card.

I picked it up, opened it and saw that it was signed by several people. With a bit of close peering and guess work, I made out the signatures to be those of Izabel and Paulo Roberto Santos, Ricardo and Rosimar Santos, Flavia Santos and Maria and Luis Fernando de Souza and their children – at least thought that was what was written after the last name. But most exciting of all was the fact that there was an address at the bottom of the card. I phoned Suzan and Jim straight away to tell them what I had found. A card coming from people in Brazil to my old uncle on his hundredth birthday in 1981, sixty-five years after he had left Brazil in 1916, must have some very strong tie to a special friendship he had had with these people's families.

As you can imagine, I was round the next day at Suzana and Jim's house to show them the card and to get a translation from Suzana of what had been hand-written on the card above the signatures, just below the big florid print of what I presumed to be a standard Portuguese birthday greeting. It didn't say much, but what it did say was enough to whet my appetite to know more. This is how Suzana translated it:

> May God bless you a thousand times over. Your kindness to our family will never be forgotten. We will hold you in our hearts for ever.

'It's got to have something to do with Pedro,' I said.

'Or the girl maybe,' said Suzana

'Yes, that's true, but I think Pedro's the connection,' I replied, all fired up to find out more.

It was twenty-seven years since that birthday card had been sent and there was every likelihood that the address on the card was now obsolete – presumably people in Brazil moved house from time to time in much the same way as we do, I thought. But I decided it was worth trying to make contact, and Suzana agreed to write a letter explaining who I was and how much I wanted to know something about my late old uncle's life in Brazil and his contact with their family or families and so on.

'You might as well write it to the first people who have signed the card,' I said.

So it was that a letter went off to Izabel and Paulo Roberto Santos at a place called Maringá in the west of Parana. After that, it was just a matter of waiting. I did, of course, get in touch with my parents who were very interested in it all. My mother had the grace to acknowledge with a laugh that it was as well the cardboard box had come my way or else this detective trail would have been 'snuffed out before it had even started' as she put it.

Looking at the date as I write this – because the letter is before me at the moment – I would calculate that the eagerly awaited reply was written probably about three or four days after Suzana's letter got there – allowing, let's say, five days to make the journey. I did that little calculation because I like doing that sort of thing, but also to show you that the recipients didn't delay. They replied more or less straight away and that spoke volumes in itself to me, even before I read their letter, about how important old Uncle John was to them. Perhaps I shouldn't have been too surprised about that, since they had written on the birthday card 'we will hold you in our hearts for ever'.

There were in fact two letters. One was in Portuguese and was addressed to Suzana – presumably acknowledging the fact that she had written to them on my behalf. I gave that letter to her straight away. The other letter was to me, written in English. Both were from Flavia Santos. I was delighted that I could read directly what Flavia had to say, without having to get it translated. It made it all very personal and I warmed to the letter right away.

Flavia, so she told me, was the great granddaughter of Pedro – full name Joao Pedro de Souza, apparently. Her grandparents to whom Suzana and I had addressed the letter had died in the late 1980s, just a few years after signing that birthday greetings card for old Uncle John. Her grandmother, Izabel, had been Pedro's daughter and the Luis Fernando de Souza who had also signed the birthday card was her grandmother's younger brother. Ricardo and Rosimar Santos were Flavia's parents. I got a bit confused reading all this and had to get out a pen and put it all down on paper.

Without going into much detail, Flavia said that old Uncle John had been of tremendous help to the Pedro family over the years, especially when Pedro and his wife died in some epidemic in 1930, leaving nineteen-year-old Izabel to look after her five-year-old brother Luis and her two-year-old sister Ana. Even when Izabel married Roberto three years later, regular financial support continued to come to them from old Uncle John. Without that help and that kindness, Flavia said, her grandmother had often told her that life would have been impossible for them.

They were not a rich family. The amazing thing was that the help didn't stop in the 1930s, but went on year after year, with Flavia herself benefiting from it right through until the late 1970s when she had gone to university in Curitiba. It seemed to have been a life-long commitment by old Uncle John. If only that could have been said at his funeral, but no one seemed to know about it, not even my own grandmother, his niece. Old Uncle John's kindness had been a quiet, secret sort of thing, although presumably his wife, my grandmother's aunt, was aware of what was going on.

Well, I read all this with interest, of course, only to find that the end of the letter brought the greatest surprise. Apparently, old Uncle John had left quite a lot of money in his will for the setting up of a day nursery-cum-orphanage in a small town a little further to the west of Maringá, quite near to the river Parana that runs down the western border of Brazil. This had been built in 1990 and had been going for eighteen years by now. It was called the 'Home of Kindness'. Old Uncle John had apparently stipulated in his will that his name should not figure in the name of the nursery, something which Flavia said her family had been keen to do. And then came the bit in the letter that set me thinking – 'I do not know your situation, but if you could ever come out to Brazil and visit us and see this thing that your uncle did for us, we would be delighted to welcome you.'

By now I was half living in Brazil in my mind. It was as though I had been standing near a door that I had hardly noticed, only to have the door swing open, wide enough for me to see through into another world. I felt that there was still so much to know about what I had come to call 'the Pedro story'. It also crossed my mind that maybe the 'Pedro family' were hoarding some letters from Uncle John to Pedro – unlikely after all these years, but just possible, I thought.

I have the kind of job where things are fairly flexible, so I don't suppose you are surprised to learn that, four weeks after getting Flavia's letter, I was on my way to Brazil. My parents said that they were long past influencing what I did and although they let slip on one or two occasions that they thought the journey wasn't really necessary, they wished me well and told me to remember to take plenty of photos. Suzana and Jim were very positive and Suzana in particular was full of little bits of advice about the journey – what to do and what not to do etc. She had never been to Maringá, but knew where it was and was sure that I would like that western part of Paraná.

So it was, that after a busy four weeks, I took off from London Heathrow on a plane going to Sao Paulo, not a little excited about making the long journey and wondering what would make of it all once it was over.

At Sao Paulo I got a flight down to Curitiba and put up in a hotel near the airport, recommended to me by Flavia who had written several times since that first letter of hers. She told me in these letters how much everybody was looking forward to seeing me and of how there would be quite a family welcome waiting for me. I was a bit nervous about that, since it was not as though I was old Uncle John come back in the flesh to be feted, but at the same time I was looking forward to it all. I took a day in Curitiba to get over jet lag before getting a long-distance and very comfortable bus to take me to Maringá. I phoned Flavia from Curitiba and heard her voice for the first time – splendid English with an attractive Portuguese accent to it. I wondered what she looked like.

Flavia and her father Ricardo were there to meet me at the bus station with their warm Brazilian embraces. My eyes blinked a little at this effusiveness, but Suzana had warned me that this was normal practice and that I would just have to get used to it.

From the bus station we drove to a rather nice house at the address to which Suzana and I had sent our first letter. Ricardo and his wife Rosimar had moved into this house after the death of his parents. It was then I learned that Flavia did not live in Maringá. When I asked her where she did live, she smiled and said, 'Can you guess?' and told me that she ran the day nursery and orphanage that old Uncle John had enabled them to build and operate. 'So thanks to your Uncle I've got a job,' she said with a laugh.

It seemed that all the world and his wife were there at Ricardo's house to welcome me. Apart from Flavia, one or two others had some English, which they were glad to prac- se on me, but when speaking to most people I needed Flavia by my side to interpret for me. The oldest person there was Luis Fernando de Souza, Pedro's son and the brother, you will

131

remember, of Flavia's grandmother Izabela. He told me that he had been born in 1925 and was now eighty-three years old. I chatted a little with him, but Flavia said that I would be able to talk much longer with him another day and that he had plenty to tell me 'and show you,' she said teasingly, without telling me exactly what he had to show.

That night my mind was in a whirl as I tried to get to sleep. If old Uncle John's name had been mentioned once, I reckoned it had been mentioned a hundred times. As I lay there, I tried to relate it all to the old man lying on his bed in the care home, saying to me in his weak voice, 'How kind of you to come and see me.'

'Kind,' I thought. How little I knew about it in comparison to what he knew. However, with all that had been said at the family gathering, I was not much further on in finding out about the girl or about what actually happened back there on that day when she had been shot by Pedro.

The next few days went by in a bit of a whirl. Flavia said that she had taken some holiday so as to be with me and interpret for me. I was very grateful for that and, I have to admit I enjoyed her company. I guessed that she was in her late thirties. She had never married, something which surprised me a bit because she was a very attractive woman. Anyway, she showed me around Maringá and we visited some of the members of the extended family in their own homes. Flavia was an only child. In fact, her position in the family was rather like mine, because her father's only sister had died rather suddenly at the age of fifty-eight, so it looked as though the line from Pedro, through her grandmother Izabela, was going to die out. This was not so in the case of Luis Fernando, her great uncle. His children and grandchildren seemed to be legion. I gave up trying to work out all the relationships and recording all their names.

I had a long session with Luis Fernando on the third day after my arrival in Maringá. Flavia, of course, was with me to interpret. Ever since meeting Luis at Ricardo's house, I had been looking forward to this encounter. We sat on the veranda of his house, where he insisted on introducing me to the maté green tea that was traditional to Parana and the southern gaucho states. It wasn't much to my liking, I must confess. However, it was his conversation and not his provision of drinks that interested and captivated me.

He told me that his father, Pedro, had come out of prison in 1923 and rejoined his wife Julia and his twelve-year-old daughter Izabel, who had been born not long before the José Maria uprising started in 1912. Luis had arrived in the family a couple of years after his father returned home, with Ana, his other sister, appearing on the scene three years later in 1928. He had never really known his father, but he could just remember him as a quiet, withdrawn sort of man. It was the older Izabela who had had clear memories of him, of course, and she had shared these with Luis over the years.

'After my parents' deaths in 1930, Izabela really became our mother,' said Luis. She had told him that their father's years in prison had taken their toll both physically and emotionally. Once when Izabela was about eighteen – a year before his death – Pedro had set Izabela down one day and told her why he had gone to prison. 'It was a tragedy,' he had said, 'I was just so enraged by the battle that we were losing that day, that when I saw a foreigner standing there in the open, outside one of the railway houses, I fired at him almost without thinking. I doubt if I really saw the young girl, but she was the one that got shot, thanks to my unsteady hand and poor aim.' Pedro had gone on to tell Izabela that he remembered seeing the girl collapse into the arms of the foreigner. He said that he would never forget the almost animal cry of anguish, despair and rage that came from the man. Luis paused at that point in the story and I tried to get my mind round this new picture of old Uncle John as the wounded, raging, despairing animal. This was not the kindly, gracious, old Uncle John that I had met so far in my researches.

Luis resumed talking and told me that Pedro had been very lucky to get off with his life – 'which was just as well for my existence,' he added with a smile. Pedro's actual trial did not take place for some time after his arrest, but by 1913 he was well and truly behind bars.

'Don't you know anything about what happened to my old Uncle John immediately after the shooting?' I asked.

'Yes, as it happens, I do,' said Luis. He asked Flavia to bring out on to the veranda an envelope that was lying on a table inside the house. I could just see it from where I was sitting. Flavia handed it to her great uncle, turning to me at the same time and saying, 'I think you'll find this very interesting.'

'So you already know about this, but have kept it secret from me, have you?' I said, with just a hint of mock accusation in my voice.

Flavia laughed and laid her hand on my shoulder in a reassuring way. 'Better for you to read this particular bit of information yourself, I think, than have me give you a summary,' she said, giving my shoulder a pat as she did so.

What Luis produced from the envelope was a letter written by my old Uncle John to Pedro, following the visit that had been made to the grave at Rio Negro on Easter Day in 1915. It was in Portuguese, of course, and even if I had been able to read and understand it, it would have been hard going because the ink had faded in several places. But also in the envelope was an English translation, which Flavia had prepared for me with considerable trouble. She handed it to me, brushing off with a smile my thanks for the time she had spent on what must have been an eye-straining task.

Rather than describe the letter, I think the best thing to do is to share it with you. It told me what I wanted to know. It also allowed me to 'hear' old Uncle John's voice – something I found very moving . . . and still do, as a matter of fact.

My Dear Friend Pedro,

I have just come back from Rio Negro. I took flowers and laid them on Gabriela's grave as you requested. As I did so, I prayed for you, knowing that God's forgiveness is great. I spent an hour at the grave and came away still sad, but with a feeling that I had to move on in some way. I feel that perhaps I will have to return to my own country to get a proper new start, but I will always remember you, not with anger but with sorrow at what happened. I can only hope that God can bring something beautiful out of the tragedy which has broken both our lives. It has been so good that we have been able to write to each other and I am so grateful that you have allowed me to show my friendship to you. It's very strange, but I feel very close to you and your family. In a recent letter to me, Julia told me that she and little Izabel are well. Please don't worry about them. I will make sure that they are properly provided for.

Several times you have asked me why I keep on writing to you and sending you things. Maybe now is the time when I can tell you. It has to do with what happened after that day three years ago. I hope that what I going to tell you now doesn't upset you, but I think that you have a right to know.

Gabriela, as you know, had just become my fiancée and

she had come on a visit to see me, not being aware that things were going to turn nasty at that time. The day of the battle, we had kept within the house – there was nowhere else to go to – and we had felt safe enough even although we could hear gunfire in the distance. We had just come out of the house having been told that the battle was over, when you came running by. We hardly noticed you and then it was too late when I suddenly saw you raise your rifle. I did try to grab Gabriela to shield her and that movement must have put you off your aim, because I know, my friend, that it was me you really wanted to shoot.

Gabriela was such a beautiful girl and we were so happy to think that we were going to be married. I couldn't believe it was happening when the shot rang out and she fell into my arms. I remember crying out. I was in despair. I knew she was dead. My dear friend Pedro, may God forgive me, but if I could, I would have killed you there and then, but you ran off and God stopped me from adding to the bad things of that day.

For several weeks, I did not really know what was going on around me. Gabriela's family arranged for her to be buried at Rio Negro – her father's birthplace – and I arranged for the white gravestone to be put up. It was a sad time and my thoughts were often angry and bitter. Then one day an older man called Joao Ferrera came to see me. He worked on the railroad as an ordinary labourer. I knew him vaguely as someone who worked on my stretch at times. He came from Recife like yourself. He was pretty rough spoken and I had some difficulty in making out his accent. He said that he had been watching me and felt sorry for me and that he wanted to give me an *abraço*, an embrace. At the same time, he wanted me to know that his wife had died two years previously in childbirth, along with the newborn baby. I will never forget these words that he spoke to me: 'I have learned that God's kindness never ends.' That's what he said. He didn't explain that very much. He just said the words and left.

After that visit, I took to reading my Bible and underlining the bits that confirmed what Joao Ferrera had said and I began to feel more at peace with myself and with people around me. I even began to think less angrily about you. Later when I heard that you had been sent to the prison where you are now, I made up my mind to make contact with you. Over these last two-and-a-half years, it has helped me so much to have had the opportunity of helping you and your family . . .

The letter went on from there in a lighter vein, dealing with some news about what old Uncle John was doing at that moment and hoping that the gift of food and a book would get through to Pedro all right. But I had read enough at that point and, if I am being frank with you, I felt a tear forming in my eye. I glanced at Luis and Flavia, who had remained silent as I read, and with my eyes fixed on the letter because I didn't dare look at them directly at that point, I said quite simply, 'Thank you. This is a beautiful letter.'

The conversation with Luis continued after that, as he told me what old Uncle John had meant to them as a family. His sister Izabela had told him that money had come regularly from old Uncle John, even during his early years back in Britain when he had been in the army, and of how she and her mother had prayed for him when they heard that he had been gassed. They didn't know about the Military Medal and so I told them about that.

'For us he was always a kind of hero figure,' said Luis. 'If we could have, we would have given him our own special medal.'

There was a little phrase that old Uncle John began to use in his letters to Pedro and later in his letters to Izabel. He spoke of them all as sharing in his 'little conspiracy of kindness'. I liked that phrase when Luis told me about it and I tried to imagine that I had had an inkling of it in old Uncle John's look and words to me on his hundredth birthday – 'How kind of you to come.' Possibly I was getting carried away, but I allowed myself to do so, nevertheless.

After the visit to Luis, there was only one other thing left to do and that was to go to the 'Home of Kindness' and see it for myself. Flavia drove me there the next day. Needless to say, a great fuss was made of me and I took plenty of photos to show to my folks back home, including one of Flavia and me standing under the big sign above the entrance door. I tried to make it clear that I was only a descendant of the man who had enabled the day nursery and orphanage to be built, but you would have thought otherwise if you had seen me that day being given the triumphal welcome. The children sang and performed for me, and there was a meal together. At the end of it all, I was given a beautiful plaque that seemed to weigh a ton and had me worrying about my weight allowance on the plane back to Britain. There was an engraving on it of two hands reaching out to a small boy and girl, with the words below them – 'Kindness never ends'. I looked at Flavia when I read the words and she smiled back at me with a twinkle in her eye. The translation she had made of old Uncle John's letter had not been forgotten by her, I could see.

The time had come to return home. I was sure that the contact would continue with 'the Pedro family', however. They insisted that I must come back and see them sometime. There were only a few days left before my flight and I wondered what I would do in the meantime. I mentioned this to Flavia, who said, 'Would you not like to go to Rio Negro and visit Gabriela'.

grave?' I hadn't really thought this was going to be possible in the time I had at my disposal, but she insisted it would.

So it was, then, that with her cousin Fernando driving the car, all three of us made our way south to Rio Negro. Flavia had insisted that she should come too in order to complete her job of being my interpreter. 'Otherwise, how will you get on?' she said. She knew exactly where the cemetery was located and when I asked her how she knew this, she told me that her family had been charged by old Uncle John with looking after the upkeep of Gabriela's grave. Special money had come from him for that purpose and the family had arranged for someone in Rio Negro to make sure that the grave was tidy and the stone kept white.

Flavia took me straight to the grave. Fernando waited by the car. I could see the stone well before we got to it. Its whiteness gleamed out like a light among the old stones around it that had darkened with age. The grave was neat and tidy – the man whom the family had employed must have been there very recently to do his tidying up. We stood there, reading the simple words on the stone:

Gabriela Rosa da Marques
(1889 – 1912)

I asked Flavia to translate the other words on the stone. They said that Gabriela was the much loved only daughter of Eduardo and Helena da Marques, taken from them in tragic circumstances. At the top left-hand corner of the stone there was an engraving of a clutching hand reaching out after a rising dove. This, I knew instantly, was old Uncle John's signature on the stone.

I stood there trying to roll back the years to when the body of Gabriela was lowered into the grave. I could see old Uncle John there – a broken man, still waiting for the healing visit of Joao Ferrera, and reliving in anguish the moment when Gabriela had collapsed into his arms. I shook my head and must have muttered something. I felt Flavia's arm slip into mine.

I turned to look at her and I knew then, as we both looked at each other in the quiet of that graveyard, that old Uncle John's 'conspiracy of kindness' still had some special mileage left in it for the two of us.

A Painting Challenge

Hard was their lodging, homely was their food,
For all their luxury was doing good
Sir Samuel Garth in Claremont

Surely goodness and mercy shall follow me
All the days of my life
Psalm 23

Her name was Florence or Flo, depending on how official things were. When she was on her way to church on a Sunday wearing her best dress and her white shoes – the ones she kept in a box on the shelf in her bedroom during the week – she looked a regal sort of person and was appropriately addressed as Florence by all but her closest friends. The walk to church was a dignified walk, not to be hurried. Her broad-brimmed, cream-coloured hat, with the red ribbon attached to it, sat on her head with as much dignity and splendour as any jewelled crown ever did on the head of a queen on a state occasion.

On other days, 'Flo' was the right way to address her and she wouldn't have thanked you for calling her 'Florence'. The reason, of course, was that she didn't feel a Florence kind of person from Monday to Saturday. Selling fruit and one or two touristy sort of things at a beach vending stall was a 'Flo' occupation, whereas going to church to take up her seat, third back from the front and two in from the aisle beside her friend Dorsey, was a 'Florence' moment.

The painting thing stood on the borderline between 'Flo' and 'Florence'. If it really came off, then it would probably be attributed to Florence, but as it stood at the moment, it hadn't yet stepped over the boundary around Flo and her Monday to Saturday life. The painting thing was an extremely unexpected arrival in Flo's life, not that she had never seen a picture being painted, of course, because she had seen lots of visitors to the beach hard at it on many a day. They would emerge eagerly from their hotels in the morning, armed with sketch pads, their satchels packed with drawing materials. Their objective was a shady bit under one of the trees that lined the beach. They would sit down there and begin to draw or paint, some of them even setting up a board and easel. The view of the tropical beach seemed to fascinate them. Poor things, Flo would think to herself, this must seem like heaven to them. She herself wouldn't have called it heaven, having to be at the beach every day eking out an existence selling fruit and nick-nacks, but she had a brother in Birmingham in England who had told her about the rain and grey skies there, so she could imagine how the visitors felt when they woke up, most days, to sunshine and gleaming sands with green and turquoise water to plunge into. She only saw what the visitor artists produced for all their peering at the beach and their busy concentration over their pads or boards, when they stopped at her stall before making their way back to their hotels. The drawings and paint-ings seemed very impressive to her on the whole, although there were one or two odd-looking ones. Certainly it never crossed her mind to do any painting herself, not even if she had had the money to buy all the equipment – which, of course, she didn't.

Things changed with the visit of Mr Henry Carpenter. Whatever he was, Flo thought, he wasn't a carpenter – not with those hands of his. The carpenters that Flo knew all had powerful-looking hands used to hammering and chiselling, with the almost inevitable carpenter's badge of a bashed finger, silent witness to a misplaced hammer blow. In contrast, Mr Henry Carpenter's hands were rather bony and thin, covered by a leathery sort of skin that had seen too much sun. They had probably never held a chisel, but they had certainly held a paint brush or two in their time and made good use of them. Mr Henry Carpenter's pictures were among those that Flo was able to sneak a view of when he came to buy some of her bananas – something he did every day during his two weeks' holiday. She liked what she saw.

Mr Henry Carpenter, Flo observed, was a methodical kind of person. Her friend Dorsey, with whom Flo discussed most things during the week and sometimes even during a whispered exchange in church on a Sunday, said that artists were usually an ill-disciplined lot of people. 'Bohemian,' she said with a definite nod of her head. It was a word she had read in a newspaper article about Picasso and although she wasn't sure of its exact meaning, it sounded right. But the word didn't seem to fit Mr Henry Carpenter, in Flo's estimation. In any case, his paintings weren't anything like those of Picasso, as far as Flo could see from a quick view of them. Not, of course, that she knew much about Picasso. Dorsey had said that the newspaper article she had read had been accompanied by a photo of one of Picasso's paintings and it was 'all mashed up' – a disgrace and not the sort of thing she would ever let cross the door of her house. Mr Henry Carpenter's paintings, Flo could see, were definitely not 'all mashed up'. The sea was there and the beach and the sun and that sort of thing, with lovely colours. Flo would have been quite happy to have one of them in her house.

Well, Flo never did have one of those sort of paintings by Mr Henry Carpenter in her house. He never offered her one and she wouldn't have dreamed of asking him for one, even although they became quite friendly as a result of his frequent visits to her stall. In the end, of course, he did give her something that set lots of people talking and created quite a stir but we mustn't rush things.

The exact time when Flo was ready for business varied from day to day. Usually she had to do her own buying of fruit and that could take time, depending on what was available from her sources of supply. The touristy nick-nacks she stored in a

144

padlocked box and kept in the house of a friend from church who lived not too far from the beach, so these weren't a problem. She would add to them every now and then, but frankly there was not a great turnover in sales. The fruit, on the other hand, was more profitable, but it involved a lot of work in collecting it and transporting it to the beach. However, it was a rare day that didn't see Flo all ready to open shop by 9 a.m. at the very latest.

Although by this time most folk had been up and about for two, three or even more hours, the visitors in the hotels, who were Flo's main clients, had a more leisurely start to the day. True, some of them would be out on the beach jogging and walking in the very early morning, but it was about nine in the morning, after their breakfast, before many of them really emerged to take on the day. The artists among them – and each day there were always a few, it seemed – would make their way slowly to their preferred spot and settle down for an hour or so of sketching or painting or whatever it was that they did. They and others would pass by Flo's stall, usually saying 'good morning' and sometimes stopping to have a look at what she had on display, although since her stock didn't change all that much, the longer a person was there on holiday the less he or she was likely to study what was there. Still, her fruit was always fresh and she often made a sale of bananas and oranges in particular, which included those sold to Mr Henry Carpenter.

He was the kind of man you couldn't help noticing, and the fact that he carried an easel and board and a small, plastic case (in which he kept all his brushes and paints) only made him more noticeable. He had been friendly from the start and he was always very polite in the way he spoke. By the fifth or sixth day, Flo had discovered that he was a widower with two grown-up children and three grandchildren. For his part, he had discovered that Flo now lived on her own. Her husband had gone to New York twenty years ago and didn't come back, leaving her to bring up two girls on her own. The girls, Flo told him, had done well at school. One of them was now a nurse and the other had married a teacher although, as is the way of things, they no longer lived locally. Still she saw them fairly regularly and they helped to make sure that her vending stall business worked.

'I thank God for them,' Flo told him and this led her to talk to him about her church and Dorsey and so on. He listened carefully and gave encouraging nods and smiles which helped Flo to enlarge even more on what she told him. He seemed very pleased that she did so. After a week, even though most of the information had been one-way traffic from Flo to Mr Henry Carpenter, they had established something of a friendship. A practical outcome of this friendship was that Flo made sure she reserved the best bananas for him when she set up her stall each morning.

It was into the second week of Mr Henry Carpenter's stay that he asked Flo if she had ever thought of painting.

'Hallelujah! What a question!' Flo replied. 'Goodness me! Never!'

Mr Henry Carpenter had just smiled at that reply and said that it was never too late to begin. 'You never can tell,' he said. 'Maybe you've got hidden talent.'

This only made Flo laugh loudly. She told him the results of her painting would probably end up as 'mashed up' as that Picasso fellow's pictures that Dorsey wouldn't see hanging on the walls of her house except over her dead body. They left it at that, and Mr Henry Carpenter went off to do his morning painting stint.

Rather surprisingly, he came back past Flo's stall only twenty minutes or so later. When Flo asked him if he had forgotten something, he said he wasn't feeling quite so well and thought a lie-down was what he needed. He assured Flo that he would be all right. Flo, who knew a thing or two about people being unwell, wasn't so sure. In any case, since first meeting him, Flo had wondered if perhaps Mr. Henry Carpenter was seriously not well.

'He had that look, you know,' she told Dorsey.

As Flo remembered it, this incident took place on the second Wednesday of Mr Henry Carpenter's holiday and on the Thursday he didn't appear. Flo was quite anxious, but she could hardly go to the hotel to inquire after his health. He was entitled to do other things than paint every morning, she told herself. So, after waiting until nearly 10.30 a.m. – long after the time that he would normally have appeared – she sold his reserved bananas to a nice young couple on their way for a swim.

It was with something of a relief that she saw him approaching her stall on the Friday morning at his usual time. Everything seemed to be normal. He was carrying his easel and board and his little plastic box. Flo smiled at him as he drew near and he smiled back

'Not his usual smile all the same,' Flo told Dorsey later. 'It was a little . . .'

'. . . sickly,' said Dorsey, 'you can always tell.'

'Yes, that's about right . . . sickly,' Flo agreed.

He put the easel, board and little plastic box down on the ground at the side of the stall, placed one hand on the stall itself just beside the bananas and took a big breath. Flo felt a flicker of alarm, hoping that he wasn't going to collapse on the sand in front of her. She took a step towards him as if to catch him, but he put up his hand and told her that he was all right. He had caught a sight of the startled look in her eyes. He asked her if she was very busy at the moment and, if not, could she spare a moment or two to hear what he wanted to tell her. Flo told him she had all the time in the world to listen. In his quaint way, he thanked her and began talking.

It didn't really take long for him to tell Flo what he wanted her to know. He had come on this holiday on his own as a final holiday. He wasn't well. It was what happened next that was the big surprise. Mr Henry Carpenter made it clear that he didn't expect to live for too long – he brushed aside Flo's protests with a gentle wave of his hand – and this being so, he didn't wish to do any more painting.

There were further protests from Flo and more gentle waving of his hand by Mr Henry Carpenter. He went on to say that he didn't intend taking all his painting equipment back home with him the next day. He would like Flo to have them, since she had been so kind to him. Flo said that all that she had done was to sell him a few bananas, which after all was a business deal, but he said that was nonsense. She had listened to him and shared all about her family and Dorsey and her church as though he was her friend. It was to a friend that he wanted to give his easel and board and little plastic box.

'I'm sure you have got it in you to paint something really good,' he said.

'He said that?' Dorsey interrupted incredulously as Flo told her this.

'He did,' said Flo.

Flo told him that she hadn't the first clue about painting or what to paint. He said this would come, and it would give him great pleasure to think of what Flo might eventually paint on his board.

Well, they talked for quite a bit, until Mr Henry Carpenter said he was beginning to feel a bit tired again and would need to go back to the hotel. He gave something like a small bow to Flo, thanked her again for her friendship and shook her hand warmly – 'His hand felt like the hand of a really sick man,' Flo told Dorsey, who said with near contempt for Flo's naivety in thinking it would be otherwise, 'Of course it would.' For once nearly lost for words, Flo said that she would always remember him and pray for him, and would ask the minister of her church to pray for him on Sunday. He said that would be a really nice thing to do and he would appreciate it very much.

With one of his little smiles and a wave of his hand, Mr Henry Carpenter walked out of Flo's life. She didn't see him again that day, nor on the following day – Saturday morning – when many of the visitors left for home. All that remained of him was what he had left by the side of her stall.

After he had gone, Flo was fairly quick to take the easel, board and little plastic box and cover then up under the stall itself with some cardboard from her fruit boxes. She didn't want people asking questions. She didn't know what to think, and decided that before she did anything at all, she would need to discuss things with Dorsey. It was for this reason that she went round to Dorsey's house to see her that evening. They had a good discussion and picked over all the details of Flo's encounter with Mr Henry Carpenter – his leathery hands, his sickly look, his love of bananas, his holding on to the stall as he spoke to Flo, his old-fashioned politeness, his daily addiction to painting and, of course, his final gift to Flo.

After getting over the surprise of hearing about the gift and what Mr Henry Carpenter had said to Flo about having it in her to do a painting, Dorsey was firmly of the opinion that Flo had no other choice but to go ahead and do a painting.

'You owe it to him. He's a dying man, isn't he?' she said with firmness, and that was it as far as Dorsey was concerned. What had to be done had to be done, and the sooner Flo got on with it the better. The question, of course, was what to paint? Dorsey said that if Mr Henry Carpenter had told

Flo she had it in her to paint something really good, then there was no limit to what she could paint. It was a *'carte blanche'* for Flo, she said, explaining that she had picked up that phrase from the article about Picasso that she had already mentioned several times. Flo wasn't quite so confident and they finished their evening together still uncertain about what Flo should paint, but united in the conviction that paint she must.

That Sunday Flo, or rather Florence, was at church as usual. She tried to concentrate on the service, but found it hard to do so. Her thoughts kept going back to the easel and board and little plastic case lying back in her house waiting to be used. Singing hymns, which she loved to do, was no help and praying was useless, since her mind wandered to Mr Henry Carpenter and paint brushes and colours, and an empty board waiting for her at home. At the end of the service she couldn't have told you what the sermon had been about, which was highly unusual since she and Dorsey often liked to pick it over on their way home together. Her Sunday morning at church became channelled into a simple prayer – 'Lord, give me something to paint' which was the only prayer that mattered, since she and Dorsey had agreed that a dying man like Mr Carpenter wouldn't have been so cruel as to tell Flo that she could paint something, if she couldn't.

The following week brought no resolution to Flo's problem or any answer to her prayer. She did, of course, take out the paints and look at them, but it was difficult to make head or tail of them. There were so many colours and some of them had such strange names. The brushes were nice all the same and Flo did some practice up and down movements with them in the way that she thought a real artist would. One positive step forward, however, was that she took everything to the beach on the Monday and set up the easel and board to one side of the stall. She felt that if they stood there all day, something would come to her about what to paint.

Well, it was no real surprise when she found herself with a succession of customers commenting on the board and easel. True, they hardly fitted in with the rest of the touristy nicknacks and the display of fruit, but it was just possible that Flo was branching out into the art business, so she had a few enquiries about how much she was asking for them.

'Oh! These aren't for sale,' Flo would reply. 'I'm going to paint a picture when I find the time for it.'

This raised a few eyebrows and invariably led to people asking her if she painted a lot, and if she preferred oils or acrylics or watercolours or pastels. Flo managed to palm off these technical questions by saying that she was just a beginner and so hadn't made up her mind what to use, but that she hoped to make up her mind just as soon as she had decided what she should paint. This led to a number of suggestions ranging from the bananas on the stall (a good subject for beginners, she was told) to a simple seascape (a big blue sky, blue water with a bit of turquoise in it and a sandy foreground – nothing could be simpler) to a beach hut with a palm tree behind it (nothing elaborate, everybody can draw a house after all) and so on. Flo thanked everyone for their help and said she would continue to think about it – which she did, every day throughout that week, but without arriving at any definite decision.

As the week wore on, interested people – and there were many – dropped by to see how Flo was getting on with her painting, but the board stood there untouched. More and more suggestions rolled in and were always gathered up by Flo with thanks and assurances that she would think about them. Quite a few people would stay a bit longer to chat and although she never got as close to them as she had to Mr Henry Carpenter, she heard quite a lot of things about their lives. They in turn heard a bit about Flo's life – well, to be frank, quite a lot about Flo's life, which always included her two girls and her church and her friend Dorsey. Some of what Flo heard made her laugh and some of it made her sad. She discovered that coming to a hotel on a tropical beach for your holiday was not always because things were going well in life. But with the arrival of Saturday evening, Flo was no further on in her quest.

'I still don't know what to paint,' she said to Dorsey that evening as they sat talking things over. They had lots to talk about, as usual, but this week there seemed to be even more for Flo to tell Dorsey, since she had had so many conversations with her customers during the week. Dorsey laughed at some of the things Flo had heard and tut-tutted at others. 'There's a lot of bad things going on in life,' she said.

Flo replied that she wouldn't like to paint anything 'bad'.

At church the next day – the second Sunday since Mr Henry Carpenter had surprised her with his gift – Flo was a bit more settled than the previous week. She sang the hymns with gusto and said loud amens to the prayers, putting just as much strength and feeling into it as Dorsey did. At the same time, the empty board on its easel was never too far from her thoughts and that sometimes led her to wondering how Mr Henry Carpenter was getting on. For all that she knew, he could be dead by now. She would probably never know what happened to him. Still, it was good that she had apparently brightened up his holidays for him. Poor man, he was probably just lonely and needed a kind of mother figure to talk to.

These thought came and went during the sermon. But at one point she had just slipped back into sermon-listening mode again, when she realised that the minister was quoting the last verse of Psalm 23: 'Surely goodness and mercy shall follow me all the days of my life.'

Flo knew the verse well, in fact she could repeat the whole of the psalm by heart, but suddenly these words became like the pulling apart of a thick curtain to let in the light. It was now obvious what she would paint – she would paint *goodness*. Nothing could be clearer. That's what she would do. All these people that came around her stall to buy fruit and the occasional nick-nack and who had all sorts of problems and hang-ups and disappointments that they brought on holiday with them, these people needed to see *goodness*.

It was a moment of real revelation for Flo and before she knew what she was doing she uttered a very loud 'Amen' and got a smiling acknowledgement from the preacher. Dorsey gave her an inquisitive look and Flo leant a bit sideways and said in rather too loud a whisper, 'Dorsey, I know what I'm going to paint!'

Flo and Dorsey made their way home. Now, if there was one thing about Dorsey, Flo always said, she had a particularly well-organised memory. As they were walking home, Dorsey dipped into this excellent memory, and came up with the remark that Mr Henry Carpenter had made to Flo when he had given her the easel and board and little plastic box full of his paints and paint brushes.

'Don't you remember?' Dorsey said. 'He said to you – I am sure you have got it in you to paint something really good. He was telling you to paint a picture of "good" – and that's the same thing as "goodness", isn't it?'

For Flo, this was like a double revelation – first the minister and Psalm 23 and now Dorsey with her recollection of what Mr Henry Carpenter had said. There could be no argument. It had to be a painting of goodness. A burden lifted from Flo's shoulders.

The feeling of exaltation from the revelation lasted all through Sunday afternoon and well on into the evening. It was only as she lay in bed and thought over the events of the day, that Flo began to wonder what goodness looked like. Dorsey had the unflinching conviction that Flo's painting was something of a divine commission and that it would just happen. For Dorsey, the execution of the painting was a minor matter. The picture was there, all Flo needed to do was to paint it. Cocooned in Dorsey's conviction Flo had relaxed, but now as she lay alone in bed she felt there was quite a bit more to it. After all, as far as she knew, Dorsey had never had to paint a picture.

The Monday morning collection of fruit took a little bit longer than usual, since Flo needed to pick up some extra touristy things from her supplier. The previous week had seen her stock reduced because of the increase in visitors to her stall, following all the hotel gossip about the 'fruit lady who's going to paint a masterpiece.' Quite a few people had felt obliged to buy something in return for their inquisitiveness. Flo wasn't complaining about the increase in sales, although she did wonder if Mr Henry Carpenter would have approved of a painting project generating income before it had even started. Anyway, it was a little later in the morning before she had everything laid out and was ready to open shop. She set up the board and easel in the same place as the previous week and hoped that some inspiration about how to paint goodness would come to her as the day wore on.

Some of the same people to whom she had talked the previous week turned up at the stall again. With the easel and board standing there just as they had the week before, it was inevitable that the first question these people asked Flo was, 'So, any further developments on deciding what you are going to paint?'

Some asked the question with an eye to regaling other hotel guests later with the story and getting a laugh out of it. But others, particularly those who had told her a bit about their lives, and who had shared some of their problems with her

154

were more sensitive and really interested to know how Flo was getting on in deciding what to paint.

Flo was quite happy to inform them that she had fixed on the subject of her painting. 'It came to me in church,' she said with a glow on her face, before going on to tell them how it happened and what Dorsey had said to her.

'*Goodness*,' said the visitors to the stall, either as a question or as an exclamation and sometimes as both together. 'How do you paint that?'

'Exactly,' Flo replied to them in turn. 'That's the big question, but I know it can and will be done,' saying that with a Dorsey-like inflection to her voice.

This time round there were fewer suggestions to Flo about what she should paint. Somehow, bananas and seascapes and little huts beneath palm trees didn't match up to the grand sweep of Flo's vision. The general conclusion was that Flo had chosen an impossible subject and that maybe she should think again, but that sort of remark petered out feebly when it came up against the solid and unyielding hold that Flo had on her special revelation. People went away from the stall to get on with their holiday activities a bit bewildered, but not forgetting to purchase some fruit from Flo before they went.

Once back in their hotels, it was surprising how many conversations got round to discussing Flo – not in belittling terms, but with genuine amazement at the fruit lady's revelation of what she wanted to paint. Some people said it was the first time on such a holiday that they had ever had discussions with other people on the subject of 'goodness'. Quite a few were intrigued enough to send off texts and emails to their friends back home about the whole thing.

Of course, all this background reaction was entirely unknown to Flo, who continued to stand or sit behind her stall all day, serving customers and staring all the time at the board and easel. She got to the evening no further on in knowing how to realise what she knew she had to paint. For three days it was like that and Flo got more and more anxious about it all, while her regular holiday customers began to run short of what to say to her by way of encouragement.

It all changed on the Thursday of that week. Flo set up her stall as she always did, laying out the nick-nacks and fruit in their usual attractive way – 'it's got to look nice' was one of her selling principles, she often told Dorsey. She also put up the easel and board, shaking her head as she did so and wondering if today would be the day when inspiration dawned. She settled down for the long day ahead, half day-dreaming and half watching the beginning of movement on the beach in front of her, as the holiday visitors began to emerge from their hotels. She would soon be having her first customer. As that business thought floated across her mind, she took to thinking about Mr Henry Carpenter again. Not for the first time she wondered how he was getting on – wherever he was.

Well, you know what happens when you are dreaming and wake up suddenly. It's sometimes difficult to know if the dream has ended or not. This was exactly Flo's experience because turning to look in the direction of one of the hotels, she saw the unmistakable figure of Mr Henry Carpenter making his way slowly along the beach towards her. She looked away and then looked back again, just to make sure she was seeing things properly, but there could be no mistake, it was Mr Henry Carpenter. Seeing that Flo had seen him, he even gave her one of his gentle waves.

Flo wasn't quite sure how to react. On the one hand, she was delighted to see him again, but on the other hand she had the embarrassment of having to explain the easel and board to him. It was too late to hide them away under the stall. But Mr Henry Carpenter gave no indication that he had seen them

156

Instead, he asked how Flo was and how things were with the girls and Dorsey. Flo said that they were all fine, thank you very much, but more to the point she asked, 'How are you?'

It turned out that, during his two week absence, Mr Henry Carpenter had been to see another medical specialist. This specialist had told him that the outlook was not so gloomy as Mr Henry Carpenter had been led to believe. In fact, he had been told that he should forget about winding up his life and that he should pick up some of his old interests again. A new course of treatment had been worked out for him and although he didn't feel quite back to his old self, he certainly felt a lot better than the last time he had spoken to Flo. He had decided to celebrate his new surge of life, by coming back to complete a holiday broken into by those stumbling and weakening attacks that he had had.

'So here I am,' he said, 'and how good it is to see you again.'

Well, there was no point in beating about the bush, Flo told Dorsey later, so she poured out to Mr Henry Carpenter all that had happened since he had given her the board and easel. She told him about being in church and the verse from Psalm 3. She told him what Dorsey thought. She told him about all the people from the hotels who had got caught up in her painting project one way or another. And then, with a sad look at the easel and board, she said that he could see she had not been able to make a start on the painting.

'I know what to paint, of course,' she said, 'but neither Dorsey nor I, nor any of my customers, seem to know how to paint goodness.'

Mr Henry Carpenter agreed that it was a very big subject who had chosen to paint, but it was not impossible. Hard certainly, but not impossible, was his view of the matter. He put his right hand to his mouth and plucked at his lower lip for a moment or two, as he stood there looking at the board and easel, and at Flo. Flo thought she knew where his thinking was taking him and said, 'You must have your painting things back immediately. That's what the doctor said to you, wasn't it? I couldn't possibly keep them.'

But Mr Henry Carpenter said that the board, easel and little plastic box, with its brushes and paints in it, must stay with Flo. 'You've done great things with them already and I'm sure there's more to come,' he said with a little smile.

Flo couldn't quite work that one out, since not a drop of paint had found its way on to the board as yet, and she said as much to Mr Henry Carpenter. He just smiled again and said that he was sure he wasn't mistaken in his judgement.

'Well, what could I say?' Flo said to Dorsey that evening. 'I didn't know what he was on about.'

'Of course you didn't,' Dorsey replied, 'but remember he is still an ill man and sometimes they do get funny ideas into their heads.'

'I suppose so,' Flo said, but without much conviction. Mr Henry Carpenter hadn't looked like a man with funny ideas in his head. Dorsey would have seen that for herself if she had been there.

Flo had been in a bit of a quandary, as she explained to Dorsey. One half of her felt that she should insist on giving everything back to Mr Henry Carpenter, but the other half of her wanted to go on with this painting thing. It was as she was standing there, struggling to know what to do, that Mr Henry Carpenter came up with his proposal. Although he was very insistent that Flo should keep what he had given her, he wondered if he might borrow them for that day – he would be buying new equipment the next day. Naturally, Flo agreed and so a short time later he went off with the board and the easel and the little plastic box, as though time had rolled back a couple of weeks.

'And you haven't got the painting things back yet?' asked Dorsey.

'No, he said he would return them to me tomorrow.'

'Oh well, never mind,' Dorsey said. 'It's given you another day to think of what to paint. It'll come. It'll come. I'm sure of that. You got that revelation after all, didn't you?'

On the Friday morning Flo got things going a bit earlier than usual. She hadn't slept all that well the previous night because of going over and over in her head the previous day's surprise meeting with Mr Henry Carpenter. It hadn't been the easiest of days because, without telling an outright lie, she had had to deflect a lot of questions from her regular customers who wanted to know where the board and easel had gone. She had said that it wasn't with her that day (an obvious statement), that it would be back with her the following day (a true statement, since she had every faith in Mr Henry Carpenter's honesty) and that no, she hadn't yet got a clear idea of what to paint, but she felt something was going to emerge within the next few days. So it was, then, that on the Friday morning she stood waiting for Mr Henry Carpenter. She had decided to ask him to make a suggestion of what to paint.

She saw him coming as soon as he emerged from his hotel. He was carrying the board and easel and the little plastic box. The board was turned in towards his body so she couldn't see if he had painted anything on it. She suspected that he had painted one of his pictures on it and was going to give it to her as a present. Maybe it would be a view of the beach from her stall – something to hang up in her house and look at when she was older and had closed down her stall for good. Or maybe it would be one of those sunsets that she saw other artists painting. That would look good on a wall in her house. Or maybe it would be one of waves rolling into the shore – she liked that sort of picture. Anyway, just as soon as he got to her and had given her the picture she would try to get him to suggest what to paint in order to depict goodness.

When he got to Flo's stall Mr Henry Carpenter set up the easel and put the little plastic box on the ground beside it. He thanked Flo for letting him have them for a whole day and said that he had taken the liberty of painting a picture on the board. Flo smiled, because she knew within herself that was what he had done, and that she would accept the picture when he gave it to her – she knew that was coming. He said that to paint a picture on the subject of 'goodness' was something that could easily baffle the best of artists, but for him the painting had already been done. All he needed to do was to copy it.

With that, he turned the board away from himself and showed Flo what he had painted. She let out a gasp, put her hand to her mouth and said in a voice just this side of fainting, 'O Lord!' What she saw there was a painting of herself, standing behind her stall with the fruit and nick-nacks spread out in front of her and the easel and board to one side as they had been for two weeks. On the board, in the corner, Mr Henry Carpenter had painted in these words:

My search for goodness ends here
Henry Carpenter

86 Not Out

Sorrow and silence are strong, and patient endurance is godlike
Henry Wadsworth Longfellow

But I struck one chord of music,
Like the sound of a great Amen
Adelaide Anne Proctor

It was at a place and a time when funerals were still important social events. This meant that everyone was there. You would be looked at askance if you were not at the church for funerals, no matter what issues you may have had with the deceased in years past. So you joined with everybody else, put on your black clothes and squeezed into the pews of the local church, rubbing shoulders with men from the village and with others in off the hills, or sitting uneasily alongside one of the angular, tight-lipped matriarchs of the area.

It happened regularly, as is the way of life, and funerals were graded in public opinion according to an unwritten code of practice. The mourning family was scrutinised for signs of real grief – after all the beloved, now departed, could have been a difficult, crotchety character who had made life hard for all over many years. But at the funeral there had to be some display of sober sadness to go with the black clothes. On other occasions, there was no need to muster up any pretence of grief and the whole community could mourn together quite genuinely.

Reverend John McCallum had played the leading role at local funerals for nearly sixty years. Well into his eighties, he was still officiating, standing before the packed church with something of a stoop now and speaking in a voice that had lost much of its past vigour but, as always, looking out at the faces in front of him with eyes of weary compassion. So many funerals over the years. So many tears. So much heartache. And in amongst all that were his own tears and heartache

Life had not absolved him from some of its crushing blows. People looked at him as he stood there and wondered when they would be there for their minister's own funeral service. Surely it could not be long now, because every time they saw him he seemed to be getting frailer. There was no doubt in people's minds that the grading of that funeral, when it came, would be right at the top.

Surrounding the church was the graveyard. From there you could look south and see the sea at the foot of the cliffs. Inland were the hills and a rough road, with the spread of the village nearby and the church manse clearly visible behind some low trees. Scattered up the glen were the grey stone houses – homes to some of these burly men who crammed themselves into the church pews at funerals. On a winter's day when the light was poor and the rain came scudding in from the sea, the grave-yard could be a bleak, uninviting place. It was quite the oppo-site in summer. Then, it could seem idyllic, with colourful wild flowers in profusion and no more than a gentle breeze to blow in your face or to help the meowing buzzards wheel and soar as they quartered the area in search of prey. Everybody knew that the body of John McCallum would rest in his family grave, which you passed on your left as you made your way into the church, and that his name would be added to the names of the others already inscribed on the large, pillar-like gravestone. These days, he often looked at the gravestone as a man would look at a restful place in which to lie down. But his time was not yet and he would walk on into the church, or back to the manse, to continue the calling that had been his for all these years.

There were only a few people left who remembered the day when he arrived with his young wife, Jenny. She was an Edinburgh girl whom John had met in his student days and people wondered if she would 'make it'. Of John they had little doubt. He came from these parts, although not exactly from their particular glen. Local people had guessed that he was heading for the church ever since he had been a young lad at school. Not that John knew that at the time, but older, wiser heads than his would nod to each other when they saw him and see him as minister material. He was clever at school and he had something of a family tradition to uphold, even though his father had gone to sea and ended up as ship's captain. His grandfather had been a minister somewhere up north. Once that sort of thing was in the blood, it was bound to come out again even if it did skip a generation, so people said. This was the general line of thinking and it was confirmed to everybody's satisfaction when word got around that John McCallum had gone to Edinburgh University and was likely to study theology after taking his general arts degree.

However inevitable the outcome as far as other people saw it, it had been far from inevitable to John himself. True he had done well at school and true he had gone to Edinburgh to study at the university there, thanks to having a father with enough money to finance him, but he was not at all sure he wanted to follow in his grandfather's footsteps. Not sure, that is, until in a restless mood one day at home, he picked up the small, dog-eared Bible that had belonged to his grandfather. It was something of a family heirloom which had been passed down to his grandfather from his grandfather. From time to time it would be produced and handed to visitors to the house to admire and wonder over.

As John would tell the story later on in his life – something which he did regularly as he got older – he was going though a period of doubt and uncertainty about many things. Time had changed since this copy of the Bible had first been prized and read. There was a turmoil of new ideas and thinking a around, and at university he had been exposed to them a

164

Not quite knowing why he did so, he took the Bible off the shelf where it lay and opened it. The printing was very small and difficult to read, but what impressed John was not the actual text of the Bible, but the words written on the fly-leaf by some distant ancestor of his more than a hundred and fifty years previously:

Be thou faithful unto death and I will give thee a crown of life

John would tell people that it was in reading these words that he had became certain about what he should do in life. He would be a minister, trusting God to steer him a way through his doubts and questions to a place of rock-solid security and assurance.

The nobility of a lifetime of service of God and of people glowed before him like a jewel to be grasped, is how he used to put it when he told the story. Fifty years and more on and still conducting funerals in front of the children and grand-children of his first parishioners, he remained a minister and, as everyone was ready to say, a faithful one at that. But it had not been easy.

From the start, he set out to get to know the people in his parish even better than he did already and he visited them all in their homes. He was received cautiously as befitted his status as minister. Young though he was, he was still the minister and his visit to a person's house was something of an occasion. He was careful not to be too intrusive in his questions, but things came out in intimate conversations which added a lot more colour and many hitherto unknown details to his knowledge of the community. He began to be the bearer of many confi-dences. This increased people's respect for him but, at the same time, it tended to set him apart from others. Many a time he wished it was otherwise, especially when he detected a sudden switch in people's demeanour when he met them. But he accepted that as part of his calling and put up with it.

However, when Jenny gave birth to their first child, Donald, it was almost as though people felt that the family was now one of their own and the subsequent births of Angus, Margaret, Annie and Archie made the bond with others seem even closer and tighter. There was a reassuring normality about having a family of young children around the manse, which helped to humanise the minister. He could always be asked, 'And how's Donald or Angus getting on?' and so establish a conversation with a bit of shared common experience to it. Since his children played with the other children every day and got into the same scrapes as others and since they fidgeted in the pew on a Sunday as much as children of non-ministerial families, it was clear that the minister was living through the same sort of family ups-and-downs as everybody else. Ten years into his ministry, his position in the locality had long since become secure and people spoke of 'our minister' with respect and affection, mingled with a bit of pride that they had managed to get him in the first place.

By then, on a Sunday, he found that his preaching had lost some of its initial cleverness coming from his university and college days, and had taken on a simpler, more direct garb. As he sat preparing his sermons at home in his study, he would let his mind dwell on the people who would be listening to him and this tended to be reflected in the way he approached his subject. He tried to tie down what he had to say to the daily life of his hearers and his congregation appreciated that approach. 'His preaching is improving,' they said, when the minister came up in conversation. 'He says it as it is,' they would add, which was praise indeed.

This high rating in people's estimation of him was reinforced by the way that he conducted funerals. He prepared carefully for each one, trying to make sure that he captured something of the real person in the things he said about the deceased. People went to funerals confident that justice would be done to the memory of the departed. This was true even in his early years among them, but it became even more noticeable after the death of the manse's fourth child, Annie, only a few weeks after she was born. From then on, it was said, he seemed to have an even keener sense of other people's grief and mourning. His faith consoled him, but his awareness of life's unexpected tragedies was deepened. This helped to trim off any residual, easy-going platitudes in the comfort that he brought to others. The arrival of Archie, two years or so after Annie's death, was a special consolation to John and Jenny and was welcomed by everybody as 'no more than they deserved' – though this was not how John or Jenny would have put it.

When life became especially hard, either through bereavement or disappointment or loss of some kind, it was to the minister that people turned. He never let them down. He would make his way to their houses at all hours, bringing with him a quiet peace as he spoke and prayed with them, before his return home to the welcome of Jenny and the four children. They were his delight for which he thanked God, but not without a slight tremor of fleeting anxiety, as he looked into the future and wondered what life held in store for them all.

On the twenty-fifth anniversary of his induction as their minister, the local people put on a special celebration. He was given the gift of a new leather-covered Bible, suitably inscribed on the fly-leaf, and Jenny was given an amber brooch. There was a meal at which everybody seemed to be present and things were said that had John, the minister, shaking his head in mild embarrassment. All four children, Donald, Angus, Margaret and Archie were there. Everybody agreed that Donald and Angus were fine-looking young men, Margaret a lovely

girl and Archie just like his father was at the age of sixteen –
maybe another minister in the making

A month after that happy celebration in July 1914, war broke
out. Things were never the same again.

Both Donald and Angus were among the early volunteers
to join the army, caught up by the prevailing mood of patri-
otism that was around in the early years of the war. As a
trained engineer, at the age of twenty-five Donald found himself
despatched to Chatham to the School of Military Engineering
– a branch of the army still relatively small, before the nature
of the unfolding struggle between the European powers was
adequately understood by politicians and generals, and the role
of engineers properly affirmed. By early 1915 Donald found
himself out in France.

Trench warfare was beginning to establish itself as the way
the war would be fought and the special contribution that the
Royal Engineers, or Sappers, could provide had just started to
be recognised as crucially important to the military campaign.
As one of the few really qualified engineers, Donald was in
great demand for his expertise. He wrote home with enthusiasm about the challenges he faced. He said little about the
dangers.

Angus, now approaching his twenty-third birthday, had been
working in a lawyer's office as a trainee, but quickly changed
all that to join the Argyll and Sutherland Highlanders as an
infantryman. He was posted first to Dunoon and then to various
other locations, before being allocated to a training role. At
home, Angus had often helped a local gamekeeper over the
summer and autumn, and had earned the reputation as being
something of a crack shot. It surprised nobody to hear that
he had became a rifle instructor, at a time when the army was
increasing rapidly in size and was being flooded by raw recruits
in need of training. He wrote home that he would like to b

out there in France with Donald and that he hoped to go there before too long.

Margaret, at the age of twenty, was at home nursing her own special anxieties about Malcolm Chisholm, a young man from a small town a few miles away whom she hoped would not go off to the army. Archie fretted that he was still too young to be able to go and join his brothers.

John and Jenny took the news of their sons' enlistment with calm resignation. As they said to each other many times, 'This is happening to many families in the parish and we must set an example of how to conduct ourselves.' But, while never forgetting to pray for their boys each day, they said this with an undercurrent of anxiety, breathing more easily when a reassuring letter arrived.

As the weeks went by in the latter part of 1914, news filtered back home of what was happening in France and it was very upsetting. It seemed only a matter of time before a local family would be plunged into grief over the death of a son. And so it happened. The MacVicar family was the first to go through the experience of receiving a government telegram telling them that their son had been killed in action. John was with them within an hour of the telegram arriving, consoling the broken mother and the tight-lipped father, seeing himself in their place and wondering if the faith that he spoke about to the bereaved family would be strong enough for him and Jenny if Donald or Angus should go. 'At least Angus is not in France,' he thought, and instantly felt guilty about thinking in this way in the midst of the MacVicars' grief.

This thought returned many times, however, even during the moving and dignified memorial service that he conducted in the church a few weeks later. There was no body and no coffin, so it made it all seem a bit strange, but he and the MacVicar family felt that there should be a church service.

The church was packed, as usual, and John and Jenny were not the only ones there trying to keep a hold on their vivid imagination about what might happen to their own offspring. Ian MacVicar died 'courageously', said the letter from his officer, 'doing his duty as a loyal soldier should to his King and country', 'killed instantly with no suffering', 'a credit to his regiment', 'a true martyr for the cause of peace and justice'. At the family's request, John read out these words, trying not to betray in his voice his own suspicion that Ian MacVicar's death had probably not been a very noble or pain-free thing at all. Some news from France, which was getting in to newspapers at that time, mainly in quotes from letters posted back home by soldiers, depicted confusion and disarray and pointless loss of life. There seemed to be little about it that was heroic.

As John made his ministerial round of pastoral visits and stood in the pulpit on a Sunday looking down at his parishioners, he could sense the strength of the bond that he now had with people. Not much was said, but his eyes and the eyes of others had only a thin protecting veil to hide their shared, pulsating anxiety from each other. Routine became an escape route from that anxiety, as daily life went on. It still rained. The wind still blew. The sun still came out to brighten up the hills and bring out the blue in the sea. The seagulls still glided in the sky. Cattle and sheep still had to be tended. The children still went to school. It was only in their imagination that people could hear the roar of the guns, feel the mud of Flanders cloying their feet and catch a a blurred vision of the dead and wounded. Getting on with things normally, and keeping a tight control of the imagination, became the order of the day. It deceived no one, as John knew and discovered in himself and Jenny and in the other families that he visited. But his calling was to be a rock for people in the community and he gave himself to that task. 'We must be strong,' he said to Jenny.

Donald was killed at the Battle of Neuve Chapelle on the 10th of March 1915, in the first large-scale, organised attack undertaken by the British army in the war. The Royal Engineers were much involved in ensuring good lines of communications and supplies. The shelling was intense from 7 to 8 in the morning, and it was in this hour that Donald died. The telegram said he had died in action, but not exactly how. The family was not inclined to press for any details.

It was almost as though John and Jenny had been expecting the news. Jenny sat at the table and cried, while John stood statuesque beside her with his arm on her shoulder, gazing out of the window. When the first surge of emotions had passed, John retreated to his study, leaving Jenny with some neighbours who had come to the manse once it was known that a government telegram had been delivered there. He stayed in his study for over an hour wrestling with God, sometimes on his knees and sometimes, as others in the house could hear, while pacing the floor.

He never said what happened in that room, but he emerged calm. People said that his hair went grey from that point on, but that could have been fanciful. What did happen, which was on everybody's lips soon afterwards, was his gathering of Jenny, Margaret and Archie to him and his moving prayer with the words, 'The Lord gave and the Lord has taken away: Blessed be the Name of the Lord' sounding out clearly. But his hands were trembling as he prayed, it was observed.

John insisted on conducting the memorial service himself. As in the case of Ian MacVicar, there was no coffin. Indeed, had they known it – which mercifully they did not at the time – no bodies had been found after the direct hit on the explosives in Donald's charge. At the memorial service, however, people refrained from trying to imagine too vividly what had happened. It was enough that another young man from the community had had his life cut off prematurely. There was no need of pretence of grief. All felt it. With eyes fixed on their erect, composed, but mourning minister, the packed church hung on John's words as though he had stepped straight out of the presence of God with a special word for them – which, of course, may have been true after that hour in the study.

By mid summer a pillar-like gravestone had been erected, with Donald's name inscribed on it. It replaced the simple, small stone that had been put there for Annie twenty years previously. As was fitting, her name appeared first on the new stone above that of Donald's. At the foot of the stone were the evocative Gaelic words 'gus am bris an la' ('until the day breaks'). Every Sunday people saw the memorial stone as they passed into the church, and it prompted many a sigh and tightening of the lips. John and Jenny saw it too, letting their eyes rest a little longer perhaps on the words of hope that they saw there beneath Donald's name and taking encouragement from that.

The months passed. The high days of summer, when the hay was gathered in and set up in haystacks and the peat was cut for the winter, went by. The boats went out to sea to fish as usual, until autumn wore on and the dark days of winter set in. The oil lamps were lit at night and in the glow and the shadows that they cast, where you could sit back and talk half-in and half-out of the world as it were, there was time for conversation and reflection in the homes of the glen. Always the subject was the war. When would it end? How many more young men must die? Frequently in all that was talked about, people thought about the manse and their minister.

As for the manse family itself, the loss of Donald had only increased the underlying anxiety about Angus and Margaret's young boyfriend, Malcolm, who had gone off to join the navy. Added to that there was Archie, who could talk of nothing else but joining up. Far from discouraging him, Donald's death in action had stimulated him. He was determined not to be something less than his older brother. By 1917 he had his wish and he enlisted in what was then known as the Army Service Corps.

The Sunday after Archie left home, John preached about 'trust in God' and everyone knew that the sermon had been wrung from his own heart in a special way. His prayer from the pulpit that day about 'our young men serving King and country' had a greater intensity than usual, it seemed, and there were not a few in the congregation who broke the rules and snatched a quick look at the minister's face as he prayed. What they saw was a face where strain and stress became ironed out into something smoother and more at rest, the longer the prayer went on. 'Like exhaustion after a long day in the fields, which drains away at evening when you can sit down at relax,' was how someone put it.

Letters from Angus and Archie came regularly. Neither of them had been sent to France and John and Jenny began to hope, as 1917 wore on, that there would be the long hoped for breakthrough on the Western Front that would herald the beginning of the end of the war. Then, just after Christmas 1917, letters came from Angus and Archie saying that they would be coming home for a weekend's visit. They did not say why, but John guessed that this was embarkation leave before they went out to France. His heart sank, but he and Jenny tried to make the weekend a happy one for them all. On the Sunday the two boys were at church in their uniforms – Archie, the private, smiling and excited, Angus, the sergeant, quiet and reflective. On the Sunday afternoon, Angus went out for a walk on his own. He said he would be back shortly. It was a dull, bleak winter's afternoon with a strong wind blowing in from the sea. He stood beside the memorial stone for his brother for some time before slipping into the cold shelter of the church, which is where his father found him later. John had guessed where he had gone. Nothing much was said between them, but it was obvious what Angus was thinking. All John could say was 'God will be with you,' and they walked out of the church and back home to the manse.

With Angus and Archie both in France, there was cause for heightened tension in the manse, but John and Jenny remained calm on the outside. John continued to preach with power and relevance on a Sunday and make his regular rounds of pastoral visitation during the week. He seemed to hold everything and everybody together, and he was watched carefully for any sign of crumbling. Maybe it was only in the quiet of his study that the barriers came down, but if so, not anyone – not even Jenny – knew about it.

In March 1918 the German army launched Operation Michael. The fighting around Cambrai was intense, as the British army sought to stem the German advance. Archie had become a mule handler, carrying loads up to the Front. On enlisting, they had asked him if he knew anything about animals, which he did, and so he ended up loading and coaxing mules to go forward even when the guns were firing. Two months at the Front had blunted his enthusiasm for the war and he daydreamed of getting away from it all and back home. His wish was more or less fulfilled, but not as he saw it in his dreams. When the mustard gas attack took place, he and his mules were caught up in the midst of it. He felt the pain immediately, particularly in his eyes, and realised that he had been blinded. It was his sergeant who carried him back to the medical post. There he was strapped on a stretcher and taken further back to the field hospital and eventually across the Channel to England. John and Jenny were informed that the outlook was not good.

Archie was brought by ambulance train to Stobhill Hospital in Glasgow, where John and Jenny were able to go and visit him. The sight of him lying strapped to his bed because of his constant pain and restlessness, nearly broke them both. The gas had damaged his lungs irreparably and he struggled to breathe. Jenny sat at the bedside popping bits of ice into his burning mouth, while John tried to bring a word of encouragement to him. But these words of encouragement came easier in the homes in the glen than they did at his son's bedside.

Archie died four weeks after the gas attack at Cambrai. His body was brought back home for the funeral. This time, the flag-covered coffin lay in full view at the front of the church. Again John insisted on conducting the service, standing in the pulpit drawn and pale, speaking words of consolation that were wrung from his own heart only by his unshakeable faith. People wondered how he could do it, trying to imagine the turmoil within him as he laid his youngest son to rest – a beloved late child, they said. It was a lovely spring day and clumps of primroses lay scattered over the graveyard, with the trilling song of chaffinches in the air as the Words of Committal were pronounced. In the sadness of the day there was something of nobility and even beauty in the composure of their minister that people found strangely uplifting – not that anyone could have articulated that, but it was what they felt within themselves. It made them come away from the graveyard and go home with more hope than despair.

So it was that the name of Archie McCallum went below that of Donald's on the pillar gravestone. Two sons now gone and the third, Angus, still out in France amidst the dangers of war. 'God spare him' was the daily prayer at the manse.

Angus came back from France in September of that year, one of the many shell-shocked victims of battle. He stayed in an army convalescence home in the south of England through until he was demobbed in 1919. When he returned home, he refused to say anything about his experiences in France, either to his friends or to anyone else and especially not to his parents. He would often go to the memorial gravestone in the early days of his return, where sometimes he was seen standing with his hands to his face. He attended church on a Sunday, but with no great enthusiasm, and even this attendance tailed off as time passed. It seemed that his experiences in France had knocked God out of his life – whether through anger or sheer irrelevance, he never said. This was a great sadness to John, especially since there seemed to be no way to connect with Angus about what made him act in the way he did. People said that the marks of that disappointment were stamped on John's face – increasingly so as time passed without any change taking place in Angus's outlook.

Peacetime brought changes to the glen. Many young people moved off to the big cities and the old way of life began to be less easy to maintain. Margaret married her boyfriend Malcolm Chisholm, safely back from the navy, and went off to live in Glasgow where Malcolm got a job in one of the ship-yards. Angus eventually married in 1928 at the age of thirty-seven, having moved down to London some years previously to work for an insurance firm. He seemed to rediscover some stability in life and this was helped by the birth of three chil-dren in the years that followed. John and Jenny allowed them-selves to be cocooned in the affection and ongoing life of their parish, slowly seeing the raw wounds of loss heal over to some extent as they did so.

When war broke out again in 1939 there was a service in the church praying for the glen to be spared the loss of life that had taken place in the 1914–18 war. As well as the death of Donald, Archie, and Ian McVicar in that war, there had been those of another ten young men from the area. No one wanted to see that sort of statistic repeated, with fresh names having to be added to gravestones and to the local war memorial. For John and Jenny, the family grave still confronted them each time they went to church. They could only hope it would be their names that would be inscribed on it next, rather than those of any of their family.

In March 1941 Glasgow was blitzed and Clydebank, where Margaret and Malcolm and their two children lived, was badly hit. No one could take it in when the news got to the glen. Margaret and the children had been buried under the rubble of their house. Their bodies were dug out the day after the air raid and brought back to the glen by Malcolm, who had been on night duty at the time and so away from home.

This time the congregation had to endure the sight of their seventy-eight year-old minister breaking down in public. 'Poor man, he's had it so hard.' The sight of the three coffins – one large and two small – proved almost too much for John, but with the help of a younger fellow minister he struggled through the service, his voice even getting back some of its old strength as he repeated the words of consolation and hope that he had addressed so many times over the years to mourning families. Angus had come up from London and sat there with his mother, looking at his father with unbelieving wonder that these words could really mean anything in the context of their family's tragic history.

Remarkably, the glen was spared any further loss of life due to the war, although maybe this was not too surprising in view of its depopulation in the 1920s and 30s. There were fewer young men and women around to be called up. It seemed almost unjust to people that of all the families to be hit by loss, it had to be the manse family. Sometimes that was said to John's face, but he always rejected it gently and refused to be drawn into any 'spirit of bitterness', as he put it.

177

By the time he was eighty-five years old, still visiting homes in the glen and still preaching on a Sunday, people felt that maybe he should retire. There were moments when he felt that too, especially when, as he would confide to Jenny, he almost had to whip himself into the pulpit on a Sunday morning. But somehow he felt that he had to keep going because the task was still an unfinished one. By now people sat in church listening to him but often hardly hearing what he said. This was not because John's voice was getting too feeble, although it was weaker than it had been in his prime, nor because what he said was uninteresting or lacking in challenge, but rather because the sermon seemed to come from John himself rather than from what he said. What they saw before them was a man who had lived with great personal tragedy, yet who had remained faithful to his calling. This was what impressed them most of all.

Jenny died in 1948 at the age of eighty-two. For two months she had not been at all well, finally going in to hospital where she died after only a few days. John was with her to near the end, not saying much but just being there for her. Everything important had already been said between them at a much earlier date. John seemed to take this parting with a sad peacefulness. Jenny and he had been through so much together that he couldn't believe he would be all that far behind her in this last part of the journey. He was sure that the separation would be a short one, and he told Angus so when he and his whole family came for the funeral. It seemed that nobody stayed at home the day Jenny was buried. John managed to pay tribute to Jenny in the funeral service in a way that brought out a flurry of handkerchiefs and led to many throats having to be cleared. People felt that they were coming to the end of an era and this was reinforced when they saw John leaning on Angus's arm, as he walked the short distance from the church to the pillar-like gravestone where the others in the family had been buried.

John was determined to stay on in the manse. Fortunately there was plenty of help available locally to enable him to do that. 'It can't be for long in any case,' people said. Before Angus left to return south to London, he and John did manage to have a talk together in a way that had evaded them for so many years. Angus had gone upstairs to have a look round his father's study, thinking that John was out and about. He opened the study door, only to see John on his knees beside his desk. Before he could withdraw and close the door, John saw him, stood up and invited him to come in. They sat together for a long time, before Angus emerged holding the family heirloom Bible in his hands. What they had said to each other remained one of the secrets of that study, although something of what happened there came out later.

In early 1949 at the age of eighty-six, only four months after Jenny's death, John died in his sleep one night. He had spent the previous day very happily with some friends who had taken him out to afternoon tea. News of his death was quick to reach all the homes in the glen. It was no winter storm of raging grief, as on some other occasions, bending people low in near despair and hopelessness. Rather, it was like a gentle evening breeze blowing round the houses at the end of a long summer's day. 'So he's gone,' people said to each other, shaking their heads as they did so. They felt that something special had gone out of their lives, yet at the same time there was a feeling of being ennobled and even invigorated by the memory of this man who had lived among them. These memories were legion and were shared again and again in the days leading up to the funeral.

As predicted, the grading of John's funeral was right at the top. The church and the graveyard could not have been more crowded, the singing could not have been more magnificent nor the tributes more moving and eloquent. Back north yet again, Angus surprised everyone by participating in the service. He did not say much about himself, only that since the days of the 1914–18 war, when he had lost both his brothers, he had struggled without much success to hold God and life together, and that this had been compounded even further by his sister's and two nieces' deaths during the Glasgow blitz. An almost audible sigh went round the congregation at that point. 'But for my father,' Angus went on, 'as we all know, he remained committed and faithful to God and his calling all the days of his life.'

He then reminded them of the story that John had often told about the words on the fly-leaf of the Bible given to him by his grandfather and, to a still and quiet church, he spoke about finding his father on his knees in his study only a few months previously.

'He told me then,' Angus continued, in a voice with a tremor in it, 'that it was on his knees that he had found strength to cope with the tragedies of our family and the burdens of his calling,' before adding quietly, 'and for that I envy him.'

When the inscription was put on the gravestone, the wording was chosen not just by Angus, but by the whole community. So it was that beneath the names of Annie, Donald, Archie, Margaret, the two grandchildren Mary and Janet, and that of Jenny, there appeared these words:

The Rev. John McCallum (1863–1949)
beloved husband and father
as well as faithful minister of this parish for sixty-one years
Be thou faithful unto death and I will give thee a crown of life

Still there at the foot of the stone since 1915 were the words that had consoled John and Jenny over the years:

gus am bris an la.

The pillar-gravestone remains where it is today and people still stop to look at it as they pass into the church. Although the memory of the story behind the inscriptions is beginning to fade with the passage of time, the stone still has a compelling power to arrest the passer-by and provoke a moment's sombre reflection about what life did to this family.

In a house in London there lies the other memorial – the family Bible – still looked at with interest by visitors but, for Angus, always enclosing the poignant memory and presence of his father standing in his study, giving it to him to keep and to cherish.

A Dove in the Lion's Mouth

Nothing is so strong as gentleness, nothing so gentle as real strength
Saint Francis De Sales

Do not envy a violent man or choose any of his ways
Proverbs 3:31

She had a high reputation locally for being able to extract jiggers from people's feet. She was often to be seen bending low over someone's foot carefully removing the jiggers with a needle. The setting was a far cry from the sterilised treatment room of a hospital, but the effectiveness of her probing couldn't have been bettered anywhere. She got the jiggers out and earned the gratitude of many.

Her name was Mbo Marguerite and the jiggers – the chigoe flea – were part of the insect life of equatorial Africa, little fleas that burrowed their way into the sides of people's toes or into the folds of skin to lay their eggs. The egg sack got bigger and bigger causing the host a lot of itching and painful walking unless removed. Mbo was expert at removing the whole egg sack intact. Her rough, work-worn hands were surprisingly gentle.

By the time Mbo had built up her large clientele, she was well on in years. Looking at her, it was hard to say how old she was. She looked like an old woman, but she could have been much younger than she appeared. There was the tendency to look away quickly, because she had a large goitre hanging from her neck which she made no attempt to cover up in any way. But once you had recovered from the shock of the goitre and let your eyes travel upwards to her face, you were rewarded by a pair of beautiful, restful and gentle eyes that held you there and stopped your gaze from slipping back down to dwell on the goitre. As for her clients, I doubt if they ever registered the goitre at all or took much note of the fact that she lived in a very dilapidated and tumbledown mud-and-thatch house. She held her 'surgeries' in the open space in front of her house, with the 'patient' sitting on one low stool and her on another, so the house served as no more than a backdrop. In any case, it was not much different from the houses of her clients themselves, although most of theirs, unlike hers, were rain-proof. The thatch on her roof was badly in need of replacement.

Others who gathered around Mbo, and didn't much notice the poverty of her surroundings, were children. She had a sort of Pied Piper quality when it came to children. They sat on the ground around the door of her house or clustered around her when she was outside sitting on her stool chopping up some manioc leaves for her meal, and they listened to her telling them stories. She spoke in a soft, low voice with the hint of a quiet laugh in it – never loud or angry or raucous like some of her neighbours, as they shouted across to each other in the course of a day. But of all the stories she told, none was more fascinating than the story of Mbo herself, although this was one she never referred to. She didn't need to, of course, because it was so well known all around.

She was a twin, as her name indicated, but the other twin, Mpia, had died many years ago. Her upbringing was quite an ordinary one, in a village where everybody survived more or less as their ancestors had done by growing in their 'gardens' what was needed for eating, or by fishing or maybe by the occasional hunt in the dwindling forest. One thing that was different about her in comparison with previous generations was that she had been able to attend school and so learned to read and write. The school in her village had been a very simple one, with a teacher who himself could not do much more than read and write and manage some basic arithmetic. By dint of much repetitive chanting and learning by rote, these skills were passed on to most of his pupils, Mbo being one of them. Having mastered what the teacher had to teach, that was the end of Mbo's formal education and she settled down to the daily round of village life expected of a young girl and woman. It was mainly uninterrupted drudgery attending to household chores and working in the family garden – a plot of land well outside the village where people grew their crops of manioc.

The bright spot in Mbo's life came once a week on a Sunday. On that day she went to the small, mud-walled village church. She sat on a bench in front of the village catechist, who took up his position behind the table on which stood the statutory bunch of flowers in an old beer bottle. Her reading skills enabled her to use a rather smudgy red hymn book and to follow the Bible reading. In fact, she was better at reading out loud than the catechist himself and she was often called upon to do so. She imbibed all that she heard and stored it away to weave into the stories which she loved to tell to the children. But she did more than that, because what she read, sang about and listened to was allowed to mould her as a person.

She never married, which was very unusual, but then maybe the early onset of her goitre had something to do with that. It was the fact that she was unmarried, however, which opened the door to the remarkable things she did over a three-month period, and which earned for her such a reputation locally.

There were two dominant tribes where she lived, with a third even bigger tribe bordering the territory of the first two. In times past, these tribes had had their squabbles and occasional mini wars, but that was a long time ago. For the most part, by the time Mbo appeared on the scene they lived and worked alongside each other without too much bother. But appearances can be deceptive and there were a lot of underlying animosities, just waiting for an opportunity to surface. They got their opportunity with a rearrangement of the admin istrative boundaries of the region. Land, always a sensitive issue, lay at the root of the problem. Old wounds of what had seemed long-buried disputes were reopened, and violence soon followed.

It wasn't long before shocking stories began to circulate and fear became people's daily companion. At first, it wasn't much more than accounts of how some people had been attacked on the road and beaten up. Then it escalated to someone's house having being burned down. Eventually there came the first death. After that it got very serious indeed since, as everyone knew, a death couldn't go without a suitable reprisal – a death in return. The horror stories began to abound. A village had been attacked, three people had been killed in the fighting and four others had been taken away by the attackers. Two days later, the bodies of the four were found drifting down the river, all tied together with hands lashed behind their backs – they had been taken out into the river in a canoe and then tipped overboard as a group. More fighting led to more houses being burned down. A distant relative of Mbo's ended up in the local hospital with a mean, single-pronged fish arrow embedded in his hand and a spear wound in his back. The spear wound went unnoticed at first, but that was what killed him in the end.

In an effort to get some control over the situation the para-military police got involved, only to find themselves split along tribal lines as well, so ending up on opposing sides. To the machetes, spears and arrow-heads were now added guns and the possibility of a serious inter-tribal war. The outlook was bleak for ordinary people like Mbo who felt helpless and trapped by the situation, yet who couldn't help but be influenced by one-sided reporting of events. It didn't take much to push every-body firmly onto one side or the other, seeing nothing but bad in the opposing side. Mbo struggled against this flow of opinion around her, but it was not easy, especially since she knew about the death of her relative. Sundays remained special days for her, but there was not much joy in them any more. Their little church building had big words painted on the wall behind where the catechist stood – God is Love. For Mbo this was a constant rebuke and conundrum.

Mbo was never very sure when she became convinced of what she had to do. Later she would say that it just grew on her. When asked when it came out into the open, however, she could pinpoint that occasion quite easily. It began with a casual conversation with her neighbour late one afternoon when the neighbour was rolling out some dried manioc on a trestle table at the side of her house. They had talked about this and that in the normal way of things, getting on to the latest story or rumour that was doing the rounds about some atrocity committed by people from the other tribe. Mbo had sighed at that point, so she said later, and had said that she wished she could do something about it. Her neighbour, who was a good friend, had laughed a tight little laugh and asked Mbo, with heavy sarcasm, if she would like to borrow her husband's fishing spear and get on with it. The thought of gentle Mbo, with her doe-like eyes, rushing at the enemy brandishing a spear made her neighbour laugh outright and shout the joke across to another neighbour. But Mbo didn't laugh. Instead, she said quietly to her neighbour that she was indeed going to try her best to do something about it, but that she wouldn't be going with a fish spear or anything like that in her hand.

What Mbo reckoned on was that nobody would see her as a threat. After all, she was just the woman with the funny swelling on her neck who had never got married and who lived in one of the most dilapidated houses in the village. So, if she said things that were eccentric and at the other extreme from popular thinking and attitudes, she could be ignored. She wasn't anybody important. She tested out the new theory, which had been maturing in her mind for several days, by asking her neighbour (when she had stopped laughing and joking about Mbo with the other neighbour) if she knew any really nice people in the other tribe.

'Did you ever know anyone really nice amongst the Batunka?'

'What did you say?'

'I said, did you ever know anyone really nice amongst the Batunka?'

'I thought that's what you said. The answer is no.'

'What about . . .?' (Here Mbo mentioned a woman who had been to school with her neighbour and with whom Mbo knew her neighbour had been great friends at one point.)

'Well, she was different . . . and in any case I haven't seen her in years. She married and went off to live in the big city.'

'But what made her different from the others?'

That was the sort of conversation that Mbo began to have with people in the houses nearby. It was difficult to be angry with Mbo for asking these questions, although it made some people very uncomfortable. They terminated the conversation abruptly with a counter question to Mbo, 'Why are you asking these questions? What are you trying to say?'

To which Mbo would usually reply, 'I'm just asking, that's all. Don't get upset.'

But some people did get upset and went off muttering under their breath and giving Mbo funny looks. Mbo would merely smile a little smile to herself. She told herself that she was not in the business of providing people with any answers. Her job, she felt, was just to ask the questions.

Word got around that Mbo was asking questions and she became the topic of conversation herself. 'Has Mbo been at you?' people would ask each other. 'She seems to think that we should like the Batunka – and that after what happened the other day.'

What Mbo discovered, of course, was that in most cases the people to whom she spoke drew a dividing line between the Batunka as a whole, who were doing these terrible things, and some individual or individuals in that tribe who were 'different' What would come of it all, she had no idea, but she felt that what she was doing had to be done. She did it in church on a Sunday as well, even asking the catechist as he stood there after the service with his back to the words on the wall – 'God is Love'. He said that of course God loved everyone, but you couldn't let the Batunka get off with murder. Did Mbo know for example, that they had burned a church building down – yes, actually burnt down a church building? Mbo didn't know that, and it made her sad to hear it, but she still went on with her questioning.

The next stage in Mbo's mission, as she had come to call it, was to move away from her immediate neighbourhood and try her questions out on other people whom she didn't know quite so well. This was more difficult and she got some very angry answers, as well as being told to clear off and go back home. But there were others who seemed to be genuinely disturbed by her questions, because again Mbo discovered that most folks knew someone quite nice in the other tribe, even though they found it hard to admit that to themselves, far less to anyone else.

It was as she was talking to a woman who came from village some distance away, that it became clear to Mbo what her next step should be. The conversation, as Mbo would tell the story later, was as follows.

'Did you ever know anyone really nice amongst the Batunka That was the standard opening gambit and usually it was followed by a request to repeat the question, as though the other person couldn't quite believe what she was hearing.

This time, however, instead of the woman admitting that she did know someone quite nice in the other tribe, she turned angrily on Mbo and said, 'If you're so keen on asking me if I know anyone nice amongst the Batunka, why don't you go and ask them if they know anyone nice amongst us, because it doesn't look like it from what they have been doing.'

This was followed by a long list of the worst of the recent atrocities, with the woman's voice getting louder and angrier the more she went on.

It was a moment of revelation for Mbo and instead of going on with her standard secondary questions, she merely replied, 'Yes, well maybe I'll do that.'

To which the other woman, just managing to hear Mbo's quiet voice breaking into her litany of the other tribe's wrong-doings, replied, 'You do that and then maybe you'll see what I mean – that is, if ever you get back home in one piece.'

Before Mbo could do anything about her new determination, she had to cope with what happened to her house one night. Three stones came through the roof while she was asleep and she was fortunate not to be hit by any of them. The roof was flimsy, so the stones came through it easily. Mbo woke with a start and an adrenalin rush of panic, but she was too fright-ened to go outside and see who had thrown the stones. Maybe it was some of the Batunka, and maybe they were doing the same to other neighbouring houses. Mbo could only hope that they wouldn't set fire to the thatch, as she had heard they were doing in other villages – they did it to a church, she thought, so they wouldn't hold back from doing it to a house like hers. Too frightened to move, she just curled herself up on her mat on top of her wooden slatted bed and prayed for safety. Nothing else happened and there was no general hubbub in the village, so after a time she fell asleep again.

In the morning, she realised that it had been her house alone which had been targeted. She showed her neighbours the stones and there was a lot of shocked tutting, although it was clear from the way people spoke that they understood why it had happened.

'You've been asking awkward questions, you know,' they said, 'and it's clear somebody hasn't liked that and is giving you a warning. Not that we approve, course, but you know how it is. You'll really have to be careful. People are very edgy these days.'

Mbo kept the stones, which seemed a strange thing to do, but she said that she needed them as a reminder. 'Very sensible too,' said her neighbour, whose husband and son helped to patch up Mbo's roof. But Mbo kept the stones not to remind her to give up what she was doing, but rather to press on with it. She looked at the stones every day and told herself that this was exactly the sort of violence which needed to be opposed.

The problem was to know how to approach any of the Batunka. The ones who used to live nearby had all disappeared to a safer place. Mbo could hardly blame them for that. If some local hooligans had thrown stones through her roof, she could just imagine what they would have done to a Batunka man or woman who was still around the place. However she did have a secret card to play. One of her cousins had married a Batunka man many years back and she was convinced that this family would not refuse to see her. She was also sure, that they had some gardens not too far from where she had her and that with a little bit of good fortune she might manage to meet up with them – which is exactly what happened a few days after the stone-throwing incident.

As usual, Mbo had gone to her garden in the early morning

She left her house just before dawn broke, so as to make as much use of the cooler hours of the day as possible. There were other woman alongside Mbo on the trudge to the gardens, but as they got near to where they would all be working for the next three hours or so, Mbo managed to make up some excuse about wishing to check up on some special medicinal plants which she thought were to be found nearby. It was not quite the truth, Mbo had to acknowledge to herself, but maybe in the circumstances she could be forgiven for that. It didn't take her too long to make her way towards where she knew her Batunka cousin had her garden. To her delight, when she got there there was only one woman in sight and it turned out to be one of her cousin's family.

To start with there was some tension, because the Batunka woman didn't seem at all pleased to see Mbo. But once Mbo had shown that she was on her own, and once she had begun to ask questions about how the family and children were getting on and so forth, the other woman relaxed a bit. Mbo managed to keep the conversation away from any of the current horror stories and eventually got round to asking if it would be all right if she paid her cousin a visit. The woman said she would ask about this once she was back in her village and she promised to let Mbo know the result in a couple of days time when she came back to work in her garden. Mbo said that was just fine.

And so it happened that, a week later, Mbo found herself in her cousin's house. She could hardly say that the welcome was effusive, but she and her cousin had enough of a family tie to ensure there were things to talk about and share which interested them both. In any case, her cousin had not been finding life very easy, because despite all the years she had spent in the midst of family and neighbours from another tribe, and the fact that her children and their children were looked on as from that tribe, there were times when she sensed an underlying suspicion in others when they met and talked to her. So it was nice to have Mbo with her for a few hours. Mbo herself could not be seen as a threat to anybody and was well-enough known locally to be allowed to pass without much notice.

It took some courage on Mbo's part, however, to ask her opening 'mission question' of her cousin's neighbours in that Batunka village – 'Do you know anyone nice in . . .?' This time she mentioned her own tribe. She didn't begin to do this until maybe her third or fourth visit to her cousin, after the sight of her in her cousin's house had been accepted as nothing too unusual.

What she discovered was similar to what she had discovered when she put that question to her own neighbours. Most folks did know of someone 'nice'. Some of them were even relaxed enough to laugh and say, 'Well, you, of course,' and Mbo had to press them to try and think of another person. On the other hand, there were some who refused to answer and looked at Mbo with angry looks and a hint of dark thought in their eyes. But one way or another, what Mbo did by asking her 'question' and the supplementary one about why the majority of the other tribe were different from the 'nice' people was to feed into the daily chit-chat of people comments about herself and her questions.

These visits to her cousin stopped after she was roughed up on her way home from her cousin's house one evening. She knew they were only boys in their late teens, but they were big and strong, and they were just the sort to have been involved in some of the recent atrocities. Further, they were probably high on drugs, Mbo reckoned, since they had their shirts open at the front and tied about their waists, as well as having the skips of their straw hats pulled well down over their eyes – the

unofficial uniform, she knew, of those who were smoking mari-
juana. They surrounded her and made fun of her and her
goitre, before beginning to push her around from one to the
other. They knew about the questions she had been asking and
told her that they knew no one nice in the other tribe and
certainly didn't think she was nice. For a little while it began
to look as though they were working themselves up to really
hurt Mbo, or even worse, until their leader suddenly gave her
a push that sent her sprawling to the ground, kicked her, told
her never to show her face in their village again and then half-
walked, half-danced away with his mob behind him whooping
and chanting one of their hate songs.

Once they had gone, Mbo got to her feet and made her
way painfully home, hoping that nobody would see her. But
of course she was seen. The story of what had happened to
her went round her own village like wildfire and became that
evening's story for the women rolling out their manioc and for
families sitting round their open fire in front of their houses.
This worried Mbo, because she was frightened that some of
the hotheads among her own village's teenagers – who were
no different from the ones she had met on her way home –
would see this as a provocation calling for a reprisal. But fortunately nothing happened. Possibly a lot of people thought that,
though it was bad for Mbo to have had such a nasty experience, she was getting not much more than she should have
expected to get for trying to be friendly with the Batunka.

For several days Mbo was more subdued than usual. The
children still came around her and she still told them stories,
but her spirits were low. It was not so much the aches and
pains in her body that bothered her – she would get over these
in a few days – it was the feeling of despair that she could not
do anything at all to lessen the mood of hatred and antago-
nism, which she was sure was spiralling up towards some violent

climax. She even stopped asking her questions and this was noticed. Then it happened, just as Mbo had feared it would.

A large crowd of Batunka got together with the regional armed police who were supporting them, and together they decided to march on the main administrative centre for the area, which happened to be located in the big village where Mbo lived. There was panic and anger everywhere. Some people fled to the islands in the river, while others got themselves armed, determined to fight it out to the end. Just at that point, however, a boatload of central government soldiers arrived, with orders to neutralise the area, stop the fighting and, in particular, prevent the Batunka from marching on the administrative centre. When Mbo heard this news she breathed a prayer of thanksgiving to God, only to have that prayer cut short when she learned that the Batunka and their armed police were not going to be put off their march. They had been seen heading resolutely towards their objective, pouring along the main road from the interior towards Mbo's village on the banks of the river.

The next news that came Mbo's way was that the central government soldiers were marching out to meet the Batunka head on. There must have been about fifty of them and they were all heavily armed. If it came to a battle it was clear that there were going to be many dead among the Batunka, despite the support of their armed police supporters. Mbo thought of her cousin and her family, and the other people who had been friendly to her when she visited her cousin's house. Afterwards she couldn't quite piece together the sequence of events, but she found herself taking a short-cut from her house over toward the main road and standing in the shelter of some trees facing an empty stretch of the road. She must have run there, although she couldn't recall having done so, because she beat the soldier to that point.

They appeared shortly after she got there, as did the advance guard of the Batunka marchers. She noticed that the armed police must have thought better of the confrontation and were not there, so that the crowd of men coming on down the road, towards where the soldiers had taken up their positions, were armed with nothing more than spears, bows and arrows, and the odd ancient-looking gun. It was going to be even more of an uneven clash. From where she stood hidden in the trees, Mbo could see it all. All she could do was to pray that something would happen to stop the inevitable blood-bath if a fight took place. She felt herself to be rooted to the ground.

The captain of the soldiers walked along the road on his own to face the Batunka army. On seeing the soldiers it had stopped, but it was obvious that people were just working up enough courage to move forward again. The captain, who must have been a courageous man, spoke to the Batunka and told them to go back to their villages because the central government was taking over control of the area. Indicating a line that he had drawn in the sandy road – just in front of where Mbo was hiding, as it turned out – he told them that if anyone crossed that line he would be obliged to give the command to his soldiers to open fire. As he said these words, he pointed back up the road to where the formidable group of helmeted soldiers had taken up firing positions. To a person with nothing more than a spear or a bow and arrow in his hand, they must have presented an awesome sight. Having made his point, the captain walked slowly back to where his soldiers were positioned, passing the hidden Mbo on the way.

There followed maybe five or ten minutes of stalemate. The soldiers kept their positions in silence and the Batunka, despite a lot of noise and shouting among themselves, made no move forward. Mbo watched breathlessly, praying hard all the time that there would be no bloodshed and violence. Then, to her dismay, she saw a surge among the Batunka and a move up the road towards her and the line on the road. Either they were going to fight or they were going to call the captain's bluff and dare him to give the command to his soldiers to fire. Having watched the captain closely from her hide-out, Mbo was sure that he was not in the business of bluffing. Unless something happened quickly there would soon be dead and dying Batunka lying all over the road in front of her. It was that mental picture which propelled her into action.

Without having thought through the consequences of what she did, Mbo rushed out from her place among the trees and took up her stance on the line that the captain had drawn on the road. She stood there like a traffic policeman stopping the traffic in the city, one hand raised in the direction of the soldiers and the other raised in the direction of the Batunka who were still about fifty yards from the line in their slow, noisy, courage-building progress up the road. She said nothing, because she could say nothing. She was convulsed with fear but somehow her trembling body found strength to keep her arms raised.

Her appearance out of nowhere took everybody by surprise. An involuntary order almost jumped from the captain's throat when he saw her – he was tensed up like everybody else. The order never emerged, as he saw that it was a misshapen, elderly woman who stood there and when he saw as well that the Batunka had suddenly stopped in their march towards the line.

For the Batunka, Mbo's dramatic emergence from nowhere was like someone appearing to wake them up out of a dream. Quite a number of people recognised her and remembered her as the woman with the questions. They had laughed at her and even felt angry towards her, yet here she was, flinging herself between them and the soldiers in an attempt to stop blood being shed – and in their hearts they knew that it would be mainly their blood. It was enough to break their momentum and they stopped in amazement, bracing themselves to hear the crack of a rifle and see this foolish, misguided, interfering woman drop to the ground. All the while Mbo just stood there trembling with her hands raised, praying to God that the firing wouldn't start.

She did collapse in the end, and was not conscious of what happened in the next ten minutes after her leap out on to the road. They told her afterwards that the captain of the soldiers and the leaders of the Batunka came to some agreement. Not a shot was fired. Her act had helped to defuse the situation and given space to talking rather than fighting. People said it was a miracle.

It took a long time for the inter-tribal troubles to die down, but everyone agreed that the process of abandoning violence and tit-for-tat revenge began the day Mbo stood on that road with her hands raised. She was such a gentle, unassuming person, but that day the victory had gone to her and everybody realised that.

As time passed and people continued to come to Mbo to get their jiggers removed – always marvelling at her gentle touch – Mbo slipped back into the normal world, so much so that people began to forget what she had done. For a while she had been almost feared because of her bravery and courage, and this had created a barrier between her and others, but it was not long before this came down and Mbo was able to go about her life without being stared at. This was so even when she went to see her cousin where, she discovered, the young men who had roughed her up kept well clear of her.

As for the children, her stories for them grew in number. Her own story was only learned by the children from others as they grew older, but few of those who had sat at her feet were surprised by it.

The Beach

Who buys a minute's mirth to wail a week?
Or sells eternity to get a toy?
For one sweet grape who will the wine destroy?
William Shakespeare
Rape of Lucrece

My son, give me your heart
and let your eyes keep to my ways
Proverbs 23:26

As soon as Motdeng saw her, he knew that he was in trouble. She was lying there on the beach with hardly anything on at all. Her skin had gone brown in the way that Westerners' skin always seemed to when they exposed themselves to the sun. Her long fair hair lay coiled round her neck beneath the white sunhat she was wearing. She was lying on her stomach with her face, fortunately, looking in the other direction from where Motdeng stood transfixed. He felt his mouth go dry and his heart beat twice as fast as usual. She looked just like some of the pictures of Western women that he sometimes saw on posters or on the covers of magazines on bookstalls. These pictures could be startling in themselves when you let your eyes rest on them, but they paled into insignificance in the face of the real thing. It was just as his father had said to him. He could remember the words very clearly: 'And don't you go down to the beach when you go to town, just to see these tourists in their shameful beach-clothes. That's not the way we live or dress.'

Of course, he had gone down to the beach and now he knew he was in trouble.

As he pulled himself away hastily from the sight of the near-naked woman on the beach, it didn't take much effort of imagination on Motdeng's part to hear his father's voice in his ear. His father had drilled so many things into him over the years that what Motdeng thought and did had become one with what his father thought and did – or so Motdeng seemed to think. Except this moment of madness when he had gone down to the beach. And now look what had happened. His mouth was still dry and his heart still racing as he climbed back onto the path that would take him away from the beach towards the town centre. All he could see as he half walked and half ran were the bare arms and back and long, shapely legs of this Western woman. This, he felt, was dreadful, more so because part of him was trying to stop his retreat and have him go back for another look. He began to sweat.

If only he could slip back home. Once there, he was sure, everything would settle down as it should be. As this thought went through his head, he pictured again his home some fifty miles away and the life he was used to there, where everything was clear-cut and his father was in control of all that happened

Motdeng's father was reckoned to be quite well off. He was also known as a strong disciplinarian, something Motdeng had accepted as part and parcel of life – you couldn't do much about it in any case. You did what your father said and didn't grumble openly about it, no matter how much you seethed within yourself. At least it had the advantage of providing Motdeng with precise guidance on what to do and, perhaps more importantly, what not to do.

As a child, Motdeng went to school every day, in uniform and with sandals on his feet. Some of the other children didn't have sandals to wear, but then Motdeng's father would have been mortified if he had thought that his son – *his* son – was attending school barefoot. At home he could run around barefoot if he wished to, but, 'You will always put your shoes on to go to school,' was what he had been told from his earliest days. It was clear that in his family there were strict lines of conduct, descending even to things like shoes.

His father was in the business of selling milk and had about a dozen cows which were milked twice a day. From as far back as he could remember, Motdeng had been woken in the dark of the early morning by the sound of music and the noise of loose chains being hitched up to posts in the open-sided milking shed that stood next to the house. The music was his father's idea – that the cows gave more milk if music was being played. There was only room for six cows at a time, so the music and the noise from the cowshed went on until the sun rose and it was morning proper.

Unless he was especially tired, Motdeng got up from his mat before full daylight and went to the pit-latrine at the other side of the house before splashing water over his face and brushing his teeth.

'Always brush your teeth in the morning,' he was told, 'and always wash your face.'

If he did sleep on and his father came across him, he was hauled up and set on his feet in an instant. 'You don't get anywhere by being lazy in the morning,' his father would say to him, usually accompanying these words with a good shaking.

On one occasion, which Motdeng never forgot, he went out to the cowshed to see what was going on and to talk to the two young men who were in charge of the milking. He must have been particularly skittish that morning, because just for the sheer dare-devilry of it, he unhitched one of the cows. The result was that the cow backed off and upset a large pitcher of milk that had already been collected. For that he had to face his father's anger and was given all sorts of really dirty jobs to do around the place. Being beaten wasn't part of his family's cultural tradition, but in some ways he would rather have been beaten and got the thing over and done with. Instead of that it seemed to go on for weeks, with his father forever reminding him of what he had done, and the loss of income for the family that had resulted from his sheer stupidity and lack of self-control.

Self-control and discipline. These were the two things tha

were hammered into him from his earliest childhood days, always backed up by the grave risk of displeasing his father if he slipped up in any way.

His father had aspirations for Motdeng that he would go on to secondary school and progress from there to even higher things, but Motdeng couldn't summon up any enthusiasm for that. Although he started at secondary school, he dropped out of it as soon as he could. To start with, his father was not at all pleased at this, but on the other hand he recognised the value of having Motdeng around the place to help him every day. In the end he accepted the situation, although he sometimes grumbled about it, especially if there was some setback on the farm, such as a lack of feed or a low milk yield. When that happened, he would tell Motdeng that he ought to have been moving towards a big job by now and so be able to support the family in difficult times.

Motdeng did feel bad about this sometimes, but the feeling soon wore off because he knew that what interested him most was being around the cows, milking and looking after them. People said that he was cut out for the life of a farmer and with his father having managed successfully to set up the small farm, Motdeng was able to slip into the farmer's life without having to start things from scratch. That was his good luck, people said. So it soon became Motdeng who got up in the morning well before daybreak and led the cows to the milking shed, hitching them by their noisy chains to their posts and turning on the music. Every afternoon there was a repetition of what happened in the morning, except that this time round the milk truck arrived just after the milking was finished, and a man on the back of the truck scooped up the waiting milk churns with an easy, long-practised snatching movement.

When Motdeng saw the near-naked Western woman on the beach he must have been about seventeen years old. It wasn't his first time in the town, but it was his first time there on his own. Normally, he would have been there buying special supplies for the farm with either his father or an older cousin who worked around the place.

This time, however, his father was down with a fever and his cousin had gone off to attend to urgent family business some distance away. This left Motdeng to go to town on his own.

Before Motdeng left home, his father gave him clear instructions about what to do and what to get and, of course, warned him to be careful about giving way to some of the town's temptations – in particular the one about going down to the beach. It did cross Motdeng's mind that his father seemed to be very aware of what you might see at the beach, and so must have been there himself at some point, but of course he didn't dare to voice that thought. Still, it lingered in the back of his mind, and in the end this is probably what led him to decide to go and see things for himself. He convinced himself that if he was going to avoid a bad thing, then it would be better if he saw what this bad thing was. The reasoning sounded good, but once the deed had been done and he had seen what he saw there, he knew something had been set loose in his life that was going to need a lot of taming, if he was not going to be torn to pieces. But there was a problem, he discovered, because he found himself thinking that being torn to pieces might be what he wanted to happen. It was no wonder that he sweated on the path into town.

Once back home where he had been so sure that everything would settle down as it should be, he found that he couldn' banish from his mind the picture of the Western woman lying on the beach. There were plenty of woman to be seen around the farm but they seemed to be in an altogether different cate gory from the beach woman. Although some of the younge woman were quite attractive, they didn't create the same mouth-drying reaction in Motdeng that the woman on the beach had done. It wasn't long before he began to slip in hints, when speaking to his father, that he would be ready to go back to town at any time and so save his father from having to make the long journey there and back. It was crucially important to Motdeng that he should go on his own, but he had to be careful not to let any urgency come into his voice when he raised the subject.

There were another couple of visits into town, but these were made by his father and his cousin. Maybe his father sensed something artificial in Motdeng's generous offers. If so, he didn't say anything, but he made it clear that Motdeng would not be going into town for some time. But if his father thought that whatever had heated Motdeng up would cool off in the intervening weeks and months, he was mistaken. Motdeng got more and more determined to do what he wanted to do. As he went about his daily chores, bringing in the cows, milking them, feeding them, checking up on anything that might be wrong with them, he was convinced that the time had come for him to do his own thing. If he wanted to go to the beach at the town fifty miles away and see what he could see there, then he would do that. Why should he always be kow-towing to his father?

Around this time, they had a special visitor whom Motdeng was delighted to see. He was an old friend of the family who occasionally turned up on his journeys and spent two or three days at the farm. Motdeng had known him all his life and had always found him good fun. He was funny and relaxed, making even Motdeng's father laugh at times and he had always taken keen interest in Motdeng. He was also a bit of a hero for Motdeng, because he had been in the army and seemed very worldly-wise, as well as giving the impression that he had long since sorted out what life was all about. The other thing was that he would speak to Motdeng as his equal and that made Motdeng feel good.

On the second day of the visitor's stay, Motdeng was washing out the milk-shed after the afternoon milking when this visitor friend strolled over to see what was going on. He helped Motdeng carry the heavy milk churns to the edge of the road in front of the house, where the milk truck would pick them up. It was as they were walking back from there that they got talking about the visitor's time in the army.

'Did you like being in the army?' Motdeng asked.

'Well, it was all right, but I wouldn't have wanted to stay for years on end.'

'Why?'

'Too much jumping around and physical jerks for me,' the visitor laughed.

'And being told all the time what to do,' Motdeng added with just a little edge to his voice.

'Maybe, but that's part of being a soldier. In any case, just because you are having to obey orders doesn't mean that you don't think for yourself, you know. Sometimes the orders run out.' He said this with another of his laughs, but as he spoke he seemed to be taking quite a sharp sideways look at Motdeng. Perhaps he had picked up the edge in Motdeng's voice, but if so he didn't comment on it. They walked on for a bit without saying anything to each other until, as though he had thought about it for a couple of minutes before speaking, he said to Motdeng that he would like to tell him a story about what once happened to him. 'It's about when the orders run out,' he said, 'and you're on your own. That's when it gets really tricky.'

Arriving at the milk-shed, he leant up against one of the hitching posts and told Motdeng his story. He went into a fa amount of detail, as was the normal way of telling stories in those parts, but the gist of it was that after a small battle he and the soldiers with him had ended up in a village where they found some women hiding in a house. They had got the terrified women out of the house and it was obvious that some of the soldiers wanted to take the women for themselves.

'Sadly, these things happen,' said the visitor. 'Not shocked are you?'

'No,' said Motdeng, but as he replied he felt a tremor of alarm go through him that maybe the visitor was telling him this story on purpose. He wondered if his father had been voicing some concerns.

The visitor went on with his story. 'In case you're worried about what happened next, I stopped any move to take the women away – I was in charge, after all. I wouldn't be telling you all this, would I now, if something nasty had happened?'

'No, of course not,' Motdeng said, with perhaps a touch too much bravado in his voice.

The visitor continued, 'We could have, of course, and nobody would have been any the wiser, but even in those days I think I loved my wife and revered God more than I wanted to do anything to those frightened women. That was me. I didn't need an officer to tell me not to . . . although I'm afraid the others needed an order from me to keep them in control.' He shook his head sadly.

The serious part of the conversation ended there, with Motdeng just managing to say something about how right the visitor was and how much you need to be able to think things out yourself and so on, before switching the subject to something less pointed.

For a little while after this, Motdeng thought that he had got over his fixation with getting back to the beach at the town. The mental image that he had of the fair-haired Western woman began to fade a little, that is until the milk-churn snatcher from the truck flung him an old magazine one day, shouting out with a smutty kind of laugh as he heaved the milk churns onto the truck and went on his way, 'Have a look at that . . . you'll like it, but don't show it to your father!'

There on the front page of the magazine was the woman on the beach.

Well it might not have been, Motdeng admitted to himself as he took a closer look at the picture, but it looked very like her. The magazine was fairly smudged and dirty, but there was no hiding the woman's long legs, with only a skimpy little bit of cloth hung low around her waist. To add to it all she had nothing on above that bit of cloth apart from something hung around her neck. She had the same white sunhat on her head, with the same fair hair tumbling out from under it. Unlike what he had seen on the beach, however, the woman in the magazine was standing looking straight out at him, a full-on front view. He felt almost faint as he held the magazine, before he came to his senses and set out to get rid of the magazine as quickly as possible before anyone saw him with it in his hand. He could have cursed the man on the milk truck, because now he knew that the next time he was in town he would certainly be back at the beach.

For the next few days after that, Motdeng was very irritable and his father even asked him what had got into him. Motdeng said that he was all right and brushed aside his father's question. His father gave him a funny look, which Motdeng avoided and the matter rested there. But it only rested there for a few days because one evening as they sat outside the house after their evening meal, his father said to him, 'I think it's time you got married and I know the girl who will be ideal for you.'

Motdeng protested that he didn't want to get married just yet, but his father was quite firm about it.

'No. It's time you got married,' he repeated. 'I was married at your age and that was the best thing for me.'

It flashed through Motdeng's mind again that maybe his father had had some kind of beach experience himself and was trying to get Motdeng to take the same avoiding action that he had taken, but he didn't dare put this thought into words. Instead, he stood up and muttered that he would think about it, but that he was off to see a friend of his up the road. He got on to one of the two motorcycles that were always parked in the covered area where they were sitting and after a ferocious kick-start rode off, accelerating loudly out onto the sandy dirt road in front of the house and disappearing into the night.

Fifteen minutes or so later, a motorbike came roaring back up the road towards the house. Motdeng's father was still sitting where Motdeng had left him and on hearing the motorbike he gave a grunt of annoyance. He was going to have to have some serious words with Motdeng, that was for sure. The sooner he settled down a bit, the better it would be for him and for the family. He was far too restless these days and driving a motorbike at night at that speed, on these roads, was irresponsible. He had already made it clear to Motdeng that there were rules to be kept when it came to using one of the motorbikes. If Motdeng wasn't going to observe these rules, then he would have to debar him from using the motorbike. He stood up as the motorbike swept in from the road towards the front of the house, ready to confront Motdeng there and then.

But it wasn't Motdeng who pulled up in front of the house, it was Motdeng's friend.

'There's been an accident.'

The remainder of that evening and all the night that followed was a series of anxious moments, first as Motdeng was cared for at the site of the accident where he had careered off the

211

road at a corner, then as he was carefully lifted onto the back of a truck and taken the fifty long miles to the hospital in the town. It looked as though his right leg and right arm were broken, but what worried everybody was the blow that he had taken to his head. He had bled quite heavily from a wound there.

There followed two or three days of waiting by the family to find out how serious Motdeng's injuries were. To everyone's relief, the head injury was judged to be not too serious, although it had left Motdeng with a sore mouth and stiff jaw that made eating difficult for some days. As had been suspected, his right arm and leg were broken and they were soon put in plaster. However, the family were assured that he would make a full recovery and everyone breathed again. Motdeng's father said nothing to Motdeng about the speed at which he had been riding and which had caused him to come off the bike at the corner and he never raised the question about Motdeng getting married. All that would have to come later, he judged.

Initially Motdeng was a bit confused, but not so confused as not to know that he was in the big hospital in the town. As he lay in bed, he realised that here he was on his next, long-planned visit to the town. He recognised the irony of it all. There would be no beach visit for him this time.

It was a well-run hospital and he had a visit from the male physiotherapist who tried to make sure that he did some exercises – not easy with a leg and arm in plaster. It became a daily routine. Then on the fourth or fifth day of these exercises, a new physiotherapist arrived to see him. She was a woman. That in itself was not a surprise, because there were plenty of woman nurses around, so why not a woman physiotherapist? But this physiotherapist was a foreigner – a volunteer from some organisation who was helping out on temporary basis. She was young, slim and blonde. As far as Motdeng was concerned, she could have been the woman on the beach or even the pin-up girl on the milk-churn catcher's magazine. He tried not to think about that as she helped him through his exercises, but it was disconcerting at times to feel her guiding hand on his arm or shoulder. She only came for a couple of days, before the male physiotherapist was back from his days off, but those two days left Motdeng with yet another disturbing layer to add to his disconcerting images of a Western woman.

There was another girl in the ward, whom Motdeng got to know. He name was Lek. She was a small-built girl about Motdeng's age, he guessed, who came into his ward from time to time. At first he thought she was a nurse, but then he learned that she just helped out – sometimes doing a bit of cleaning and sometimes lending a helping hand to patients who needed it. He and Lek met properly when she came to help him one day to get a bottle of water that had slipped out of his reach. She asked him about the accident and it turned out that she came from a place not too far away from where he lived. From then on, they felt that they had something in common and she never failed to chat a little with Motdeng when she was in his ward.

Not every day was a bright, cheerful day for Motdeng and although not a great complainer, there were times when he got frustrated. When he was like that, he was liable to moan a bit about the accident having happened and so on. It was on one of those days that Lek said to him, 'Maybe you needed to have the accident.'

Perhaps because Motdeng had been thinking the same thing himself sometimes, he was just a bit sharp when asking Lek what she meant by that remark. She backed off when she heard the tone of his voice and caught sight of the almost angry way that he looked at her. With a smile and a shrug she said quickly, 'Oh well, I don't know. Don't worry. You're going to be all right. It will just take time.'

It did take time, but eventually Motdeng got back home, where he hobbled around for a while doing what he could around the farm. Everybody was glad to have him back and bit by bit he slid back into the normal daily routine of life. He knew that he was properly back when his father began to lay down the law on some things that needed to be done, although to Motdeng's relief he didn't bring up the subject of marriage again.

It must have been about a year later that Motdeng was back in town on his own. He had, of course, been back to town in the interim to attend the hospital, but on this occasion he had come on the usual round of making purchases for the farm. He had done quite a bit of thinking about his accident as the months passed. Because his family were traditionally God-fearers, he couldn't help wondering if God hadn't caused the accident to happen as a sort of punishment. So to be on the safe side, he didn't go down to the beach – just in case.

Motdeng was in town for a full two days, and on the second evening of his stay he went for a stroll in the night market that spread out over quite an area in the town centre. It was all lights and stall after stall of everything that you could think of, including the things that tourists liked to buy. There were lots of foreign tourists there as well, picking their way through the stalls in search of a bargain. Most of the stalls ran along the main street, but some branched off up some side-streets and alleyways. It was near the top end of one of those side streets, where the lighting was not so good, that Motdeng saw her. He didn't have to look twice, despite the poor lighting. It was the blonde physiotherapist from the hospital. She was standing bent over a stall, examining some cloth that lay spread out in front of her. He stopped to watch her, wondering if he should speak to her and a little annoyed that he could detect his heart beating a bit faster. She was out of hospital uniform, of course, and dressed in a wrap-around skirt and top that clung to her quite tightly. It revealed nothing, but left plenty room for the imagination to get to work.

Motdeng was just about to step forward and summon up enough courage to speak to her when she turned round and looked in his direction. He had been staring at her after all and she might have sensed his eyes boring in on her. But as she turned to look at him she caught her foot on something, and the next thing that happened was that she ended up sprawled over the stall, face down among all the cloths. Motdeng sprang forward, as did the stall owner, but Motdeng got there first. He found himself seizing hold of her arms and pulling her back up onto her feet. For a moment, she was entirely under his control and he could feel the warmth of her body close to his. His hands tightened their grip on her, but only for a moment. She was laughing as he pulled her up and, to help her cover her embarrassment, the stallholder and Motdeng joined in the laughter too.

She had twisted her ankle a little and the concerned stall-holder got a small boy to go off in search of a three-wheeler taxi cab to take her back to where she was staying. She was made to sit down on a stool and it was as she was sitting there that Motdeng introduced himself to her.

'Now you will be the one who has to do exercises to get your ankle well again,' he said, and he told her that he knew her from his time in hospital. She smiled at that, although Motdeng doubted if she remembered him. For a few moments they chatted before the taxi cab arrived and it was all very pleasant and normal. She asked him how he was getting on and he told her that he was back working at his father's farm without any long-term bad effects from the accident. He asked her if she was still working at the hospital and she told him that she had been away from the town for several months but had come back on a visit to see some friends. As they talked, Motdeng found that he stopped thinking of her as a covered-up, erotic naked body of a slim, attractive blonde Westerner. She became a normal human being like everybody else. When the taxi came, she thanked him for his help, wished him well for the future and was gone.

For some reason he found difficult to fathom, Motdeng felt liberated. It wasn't because anyone, not least his father, had stopped him from in any way abusing the Western woman, it was simply that something had emerged from within him to change his outlook.

Some weeks later when the ex-army friend of the family was back on one of his visits, Motdeng told him all that had happened, right back to the day on the beach – he was the sort of person in whom Motdeng knew he could confide.

'I've never forgotten that story you told me about the village that you captured and these women and the way you acted,' Motdeng said.

'And neither have I,' said the visitor.

'Of course, with me it was nothing like that, and I don't have a wife like you, but do you think it was maybe God who made the woman laugh and make us all laugh with her and so stopped me from doing anything foolish? Or was it just me being sensible?'

The visitor gave a little jerk of his head and said, 'Probably a bit of both, but after all that's the way things are.'

It wasn't too long after that conversation, when Motdeng

was back in town once more, that he met a man from the village where Lek lived. One thing led to another, as is the way of things – and in the end his father never had to raise the matter of the ideal girl for Motdeng again.